NOW! THE THIRD BOOK OF THE ZAN-GAH SERIES:

ZAN-GAH: A PREHISTORIC ADVENTURE

ZAN-GAH AND THE BEAUTIFUL COUNTRY

DAEL AND THE PAINTED PEOPLE

"...rich and authentic....extremely realistic and moving.... definitely a book I would recommend for any middle grade reader, especially the boys. It's educational, fun, mysterious—everything a young reader could want!"
— *The Elliot Review*

" ...creates a primeval world that's savage, vivid, believable, and deeply moving. The author is a master storyteller, and the adventures are exciting and unlike any I've ever read before."
— *Suko's Notebook*

" Once again Shickman has provided a host of richly realized characters, a fabulous sense of place and lots of action....But in the end it is the rich characters and believable action that carry the day....A most worthy read."
— Joe Corbett,
New City School Librarian

"...it deals with the deep dilemmas and fierce confrontations between characters. The author does a great job in bringing the ancient world to life...."
— Michael Young, author of
The Canticle

"There is such a fullness in the developing relationship between Dael and Zan, and the reader can't help but sympathize with each of them....The word choices are always appropriate and never dumbed down...."
— Joan Burtelow, middle and high
school reading teacher

"This fast paced, easy to read book includes love, betrayal, jealousy, courage, inventiveness, and fanaticism....A good pick for a middle school reader looking for excitement!"
— Jessica Miller, young adult
librarian—*I Read to Relax*

"The author has painted a richly colored landscape and filled it with vibrant characters. Themes of forgiveness, dealing with hatred, brains overcoming might, and of loving another, add great depth to the story....Great material for high school students."

— Barry Crook, Library Media
Specialist, North Kirkwood
Middle School

"Shickman's prose cannot be rivaled here and I feel lucky to have read such a beautifully woven tale. He is able to take the barest of lines, and layer it with such complexity and emotion....Fraught with tension and a looming darkness...."

— *Wicked Awesome Books*

"Stunning....The descriptions are magnificent and the action superb. Young adults and adults alike will enjoy this series. I certainly did!"

— *Wendy's Minding Spot*

"A must read, and a HUGE recommendation!"

— *Freda's Voice*

"The tension, uncertainty and danger was palpable on every page....in a league of its own....absolutely wonderful....a powerful, complex novel."

— *Girls Without a Bookshelf*

"Once again Allan Shickman has blown me away....a fantastic book."   — *To Read or Not To Read*

"A new and amazing type of fiction that cannot be compared to anything else because it is so unique. Truthfully, I loved this book!"   — *A Fanatic's Book Blog*

"...each page seems to turn itself in eagerness to continue with the spellbinding tale....a depth of story rarely achieved in young adult fiction."

— *Luxury Reading*

"...an emotional roller coaster ride through the era of early man...very realistic...a great read and I highly recommend this YA series. It's perfect for the reluctant reader, providing action and adventure in addition to the emotional drama...."
— *Book Noise*

"… has you holding your breath until the end....a must read... will enthrall even the most reluctant of readers."
— *Missy Reads and Reviews*

"By the end I had run the gamut of emotions (among them: suspense, shock, heartbreak, revulsion, inspiration)....It almost felt like it was true, it was quite something....Wow."
— *Bibliophile Support Group*

"...a powerful and emotional story...."
— *Readaholic*

"…stunning and evocative..."
— *Lost for Words*

The Zan-Gah young adult series was awarded the Mom's Choice Gold Seal for Excellence in 2010.

DAEL

AND THE
PAINTED PEOPLE

By Allan Richard Shickman

EARTHSHAKER BOOKS

Dael and the Painted People

ISBN: 978-0-9790357-6-0
LCCN: 2011930497

Published in the United States by
Earthshaker Books
400 Melville
St. Louis, MO 63130

Visit our website at
www.zan-gah.net or **www.zan-gah.com**

CONTENTS

For my brothers and sister

1 COMPANIONS

To dream of a head dripping with blood and look into its glazed and lifeless eyes might, even in sleep, leave the dreamer changed and chastened. Urged and goaded by an intense hatred of Hurnoa's wasp people, Dael had wantonly taken the old woman's life, though she herself had never done him harm. He did not (the gods be thanked!) take off her head, although in his rage the wicked thought had come to him; but the hag had left his hands red and sticky with her blood. Now that blood was her rebuke. She haunted him with dull, accusing eyes and gravel speech, making sleep fitful and depriving it of its healing power. Every night, Dael awoke with a start, shaking and sweating—looking into the blackness to see whether the horrible vision still was there. Then, needing sleep and yet fearing to sleep, he would gaze into his dark surroundings and long for daybreak.

Dael was a wounded man, even if he bore no bodily wounds. Conscience-stricken and almost alone—for he had left his people behind—he thought of the harm he had done to his Ba-Coro tribe, the needless deaths he had caused, and the insults he had given to Zan-Gah, his own twin brother. He had struck Zan in the face and threatened his life! Nothing Dael had done in his lifetime, no, not the killing of the old woman, pained him as much to remember. Reasonless fury. He could see at last how much his people were divided by his mere presence, and suddenly he felt he wanted to leave forever. Overcome with remorse, he tried to understand his former self and the feelings that had driven him so furiously. Strangely, he could not even remember what they were. His rage was gone and a deep sorrow took its empty place.

Almost alone, but not completely so. At his departure he had asked Sparrow to come along, and for whatever reason or reasons—it was not love—she did. Now, a few paces behind, she trailed Dael's sad steps in complete silence; and he said not a word to her. It was not as if he was angry or sullen. Dael's mind was somewhere else, but where? Sparrow could see that his spirit was shattered, but not his strength. His pain was extreme, but his ability to endure was almost heroic. Fire and ice contended for the rule of his soul. Dael burned, but the iron grip of self-control froze him, his passions, and his speech.

Sparrow's conversation was not called for, but she was unable to speak anyway, and had been from her birth. Shy as the bird for which she was named (but not so talkative), she had not learned to chirp along with the other little birds of her clan. Her parents finally had given up their effort because they saw how much it pained her, and mute she thenceforth remained. This impairment, of which she was deeply ashamed, had isolated her from her society almost as completely as Dael's self-imposed exile.

Only one other person had ever tried to teach her. That was the great friend of Zan-Gah. Rydl was his name, a name Sparrow came to adore. Poor Sparrow! Rydl told her plainly that he could not love her or any woman. At the time he had been gravely injured, perhaps on his deathbed, and his words cost him too much effort to be lies. Even if he had given her speaking lessons, and in so doing had frequently contacted and almost caressed her lips and cheeks, there was nothing in it but his wish to help her. Love had hit Sparrow hard, but it touched Rydl not at all.

Such was her disappointment and despair that when Dael asked her (quite suddenly) to accompany him into the wilderness, she went. Surely that was not wise. It was an almost self-destructive decision, like those to which her new companion inclined. Dael was a known troublemaker, a criminal, a murderer—and quite possibly a madman as well. What safety could she hope for in his presence? Within days she might well be the dead prey of vultures or wild dogs.

But Sparrow was unconcerned about herself and, oddly, she felt that she owed duty to Dael. Good women obeyed their men, she thought; and for better or worse, Dael had become her man. She knew perfectly well that, alone in his company, he could do with her as he wanted, and she felt little inclination to resist. Sparrow had been brought up to be subservient—the more so because she was timid and unable to speak—just as her companion had learned from his childhood to take a woman's services for granted. Dael might keep her or kill her as he pleased.

But they had been in each other's presence for three days, wandering across the frightening wild, and he showed no interest in her at all, one way or another. All of Dael's passions had been stripped from him, and he had to find new reasons to love or hate. Sparrow understood that her function was to serve and take care of the empty man she followed. Dael hardly seemed to know that she was there.

At the moment they were trudging through the gnarled shrubs that had appeared in great numbers as they continued on their downward slope, marching against the sun toward the eastern world. It was a pleasant autumn day, but windy. Clouds roamed across the bright sky like a herd of grazing animals, and Dael walked on steadily, seemingly unwearied, with Sparrow behind. Each was lost in private thoughts. Dael was remembering Hurnoa whom he hated, and Sparrow was thinking of Rydl whom she loved.

Dael had loathed Hurnoa because she was of the wasp blood, but he also hated her for having tempted him to commit that great crime—and afterwards, night after night, reproaching him for it in his dreams. Had she not begged him—*begged him!*—to do it? She had handed him his own spear and bared her withered bosom. At the time, she had no one. She had nothing. Had he refused her grotesque request, she would have lain down among the rotting wasp corpses and died without his help. Why shouldn't he have done her bidding? But yet why did he? Why had he stabbed her and reveled in her blood? Was he mad? Here, and for no visible reason, Sparrow saw him clutching his head in his hands.

This involuntary action drove Sparrow's thoughts away for a moment, but they soon returned to vex her: Maybe it was always so, she reflected. The person you loved would not love you back. Maybe the only love that mattered was the one that grew slowly, slowly took root, with neither mate caring too much at first. But she did care. Love had come to Sparrow as wind comes to shake and change a young tree. It blows the leaves upside down, revealing of a sudden their tender hidden side. Love made her now a woman, now a child; but Rydl had remained always the same. He did not, would not, could not—who knew why?

But then, why would Rydl or anyone desire her? She was as plain as a boulder, she thought, or the trunk of a tree—and as speechless. She was only fit to be the servant or drudge of an unfeeling man like Dael. She looked at her bare arms and then down at her ungainly feet and dusty toes, and they were ugly to her.

In truth, her self-assessment was far from accurate. Sparrow had a pretty and gentle face with long lashes— habitually downcast. Thick, wild curls sprang from her head, and might have given her a look of boldness, were not the opposite so apparent. She was of almost medium height, her body budding with youth and health. She rarely smiled, but when she did, people were pleased and wished that she could talk. And right away she would bite her smile as if to hide it, lowering her eyelids. She was sixteen.

Did Dael love this hideous, bashful, speechless child? Sparrow did not think so for a single moment. She was his servant. She was his punishment, even, and his penance, not his love. And he would be hers.

▼ ▼ ▼

The ground was slowly beginning to turn red under their bare feet, and the travelers could dimly make out in the distance the soaring monoliths of the crimson land spread before them. Beyond that, not quite visible, was the jagged line of the chasm—a deep split in the earth. For the first time, Dael realized how gratifying was the Beautiful Country he had left behind, in contrast to the harsh, arid land he was approaching. And suddenly he was aware that he badly missed his family and friends— sorely missed his twin brother, his uncle Chul, and even Rydl who had formerly been his enemy. He thought of the many happy times he and Zan had enjoyed together before the poison of the wasp men reached him. He had been a mere child at the time he became their captive.

As boys, he and his twin were constantly at play together. They ran, they climbed, they explored. Zan had been a good tree climber, better than he. Dael recalled how Zan once had extended his hand to help him onto a thick limb, strong enough to seat them both, high above the river Nobla. After all these years, he could almost feel his brother's hand in his own. Other images of happier days returned to Dael like a scattering of bright poppies, and a wave of warm memories came over him. Then bitterness. Why had the Ba-Coro driven him out?—but they hadn't! In one of his moments of exaltation he had left of his own accord. His family had begged him to stay.

It was the spirits that had sent him forth when he visited the realm of dead ones.

Dael thought of his followers. He had had many, mystified by his powers. Two of his servants were Oin and Orah, the Hru brothers to whom he had given his pet wolves when he departed. Dael remembered his friends with less fondness than his pets. He had found the wretched, starving pups, restored them, and raised them as his own. Like his numerous followers, they had trailed his heels and adored him. He would shove them, wrestle with them, and wrench the very meat from their jaws, but still they loved and fawned on him. They could never love Oin and Orah as much. Maybe they would go wild again now. His pets had never been completely tame.

It had imperceptibly gotten quieter, and Dael turned around to see if Sparrow still was there. She was not! Alarmed, his eyes scanned the horizon behind him, swept the plain lying below the range of hills that hid from sight the Beautiful Country. How long had she been gone? She was not to be seen, not near, not far. He began to fear for her indeed. A strong young woman was always a prize to marauders, and he had been so preoccupied that he had forgotten to watch out for her safety. But to his relief, he finally spotted her sitting on the ground behind a ragged, dark-needled shrub. And then as he approached, not a little impatient, he saw that she was crying. He wanted to ask her what the matter was, but he knew that she could not reply. Her posture and color told him all he needed to know, however. She was exhausted. His strong legs carried him over any difficulties and obstacles, but she, burdened with provisions, could not keep up. He did not take her inward feelings into account.

She was a helpless thing, really—not like his lost wife Lissa-Na, who was all energy, beauty, and wisdom. Why had he brought this one along? Dael was almost glad she couldn't speak. He had his own concerns, and did not wish to listen. Yet she was his responsibility now, and he resolved to make the best of it. He had asked for her to accompany him in his exile, and surely he owed her something for doing so. So he tried to smile, and helped her with some of the load. Sparrow forced a smile too, and followed his lead after she had recovered herself, deciding that Dael was grim but not so bad as people said.

After a while, as the sun behind them descended beneath bluish hills, Dael found a place of shelter and built a fire. They had some victuals and found some desert fruit, so they ate in their usual silence. When it was time to sleep, they stoked their fire, but the wind was still blowing, colder and colder. The two travelers huddled together for warmth, as was customary. No one ever slept alone if he could avail himself of a warm body to lessen the bite of frigid weather.

Sparrow had been deliriously in love with Rydl, but Rydl could not return her love; so she consciously tried to transfer her feelings to Dael, expecting nothing in return. What else could she do? Dael could not give love anyway at this unhappy point in his life, but at least he was being kind to her. She was as vulnerable to his every mood, passion, or outburst as a small child. Sparrow lay close to her sour companion as if he were a bear, trembling with cold, and perhaps with fear as well. His limbs were hard as rocks. Dael felt her warmth and softness, but he didn't respond. But as they clung very close and closer for mere warmth, something did happen; and the next day things had changed between them. They early resumed their journey, but walked somewhat closer together—for a long time as silent as before.

Sparrow was not of a brooding temper like her companion, only very shy. Sometimes, indeed, she could be merry if she thought no one was watching—at least before she had met Rydl—and now, as they trudged along, Sparrow began to sing to herself in a soft, halting voice. She who could not talk could hum and sing, as Rydl once had discovered. Rydl, attempting to teach her speech, hoped to enlarge this limited vocal capacity. Now she remembered the words and sputtered out a few, so laboriously learned:

The w-w-wolves h-h-howl,

The b-b-birds s-s-s-sing,

And Sp-Sp-arrow sp-speaks her n-n-n-name.

What followed surprised her as much as if the bright morning sun had suddenly been replaced by a silvery moon. Dael, as if to support her efforts, began to chant the same verse. Of the two breaking into song, which was the more remarkable—she whose lips never formed words; or music from that intense and gloomy man? For not since his childhood, before his great ordeal, had anyone, *anyone*, ever heard Dael sing. And Sparrow reflected again that Dael, although harsh, was not a bad person.

Their song could not continue; it was too dangerous to do anything that might draw the attention of enemies. Dael's softening mood hardened again, and his eyes narrowed. He put his finger to his lips and, thus alerted, both scanned the large space circling them. There was nothing, yet who knew what lurked behind bushes or rocks; and so they continued on, always on the watch.

But just as they were beginning to relax and let down their guard somewhat, Sparrow saw something that set her trembling—two distant black specks far behind, where they had most recently slept. With effort she detected that they were moving unevenly in their direction. She grunted, almost whimpered, and pointed. After a moment of silent attention, as she and Dael strained to see, the dark spots were recognizable as animals sniffing at the ground and tracing the sleepers' scent. The black invaders were loping this way and that, but always in pursuit; and suddenly they increased their speed, fairly galloping toward the two unprotected wanderers. Dael finally could see that they were two large and ragged wolves, and he prepared to defend against them with his spear.

Luckily, there were only two, not a large pack. Dael had fought these predators before, and knew something of their ways—how one would attack from in front while another would tear and harass from behind. Their cleverness as well as their ferocity enabled them to bring down animals much bigger than themselves. It could take them all day, with one charging and snarling as another momentarily retreated, but together they would persist in their deadly aim until their target, wounded and exhausted, finally succumbed. A deer or even an elk could be felled in this way.

Dael and Sparrow were completely in the open. There was no large rock or tree to place at their backs— nothing but rough brush dried by the parching sun. At Dael's order, they arranged themselves back to back. Dael, with clenched teeth, was set to fight; and Sparrow, her face flushed and her unruly hair almost on end, now converted her walking staff into a weapon of defense.

The coal-black creatures were closing in with lowered heads, their terrible yellow eyes gleaming. Suddenly they almost vaulted up, with heavy purple tongues lapping between their bottom fangs. Sparrow let out a guttural scream, and aimed a blow. But the wolves were not attacking. They were frolicking, leaping and bounding joyfully in utter happiness to have found...their master. They had abandoned their keepers and followed the outcast in pure love, span after span, more faithful than any of his friends.

Dael did not repel or scold his pets as he might have done in former days. Instead he embraced them in strong arms and let them lick his face. Sparrow could see that he cared for them more than for her or perhaps any living being. She was glad that he was laughing as he crushed them to himself, but she soon understood that he was shaking, not with laughter, but with dry, rasping sobs.

2 PRAIRIE GRASSES

Only once in his life had Dael shed tears. That was when Lissa-Na died trying to give him a child. The child, his son, died too, and Dael wept. Dael was a man of war, and warriors did not cry. In his view, they did not even feel—neither sorrow nor pity. But he cried then, and he did again now. With the return of his pets, Dael was like a youngster given some wonderful gift that he never dared hope for. His two best friends, almost his only friends now, had used their keen noses, sniffing the ground until they found him. They, at least, had longed for his company.

Dael wiped his eyes and face with his tattooed fists, wondering at his weakness. He rightly considered himself a strong man, a fighter, and a leader. Only recently, fierce and ready men had clung to him, had feared and followed him. The appearance of the pets was so sudden and unexpected that Dael visibly changed. He hugged them like deep-sworn lovers come back after long absence, reaching his fingers into the thickness of their dark fur. His soul of iron seemed to melt as he embraced them; and when Dara and Nata simultaneously licked his cheeks with their dripping purple tongues, Dael broke down.

Sometimes, when great grief produces no tears, small joys will. Dael wept because he no longer had a people, no longer had family or friends, no longer even knew where his feet should take him. And he wept because he was glad—because his pets had left the comfort of their home to be with him in his sorrows. No words could express how overjoyed he was to see them.

Sparrow was frightened by his tearful, passionate outburst, and timidly placed a hand on his shoulder. She would have said something if she could. But Dael, wiping his face again, was happy now, laughing now. He had always been prone to sudden changes in mood and this was a marked instance. It was over. His confidence strangely restored, he could be himself once more. He played with the arrivals, squeezing them and making them howl while he howled triumphantly along with them so that the whole plain resounded. He was oblivious to the danger. He leapt, jostled, wrestled with them, and ran them in circles, calling them by name as if they were human or he himself part wolf. He rolled on the ground with them, stretching out the length of his body next to theirs.

When Dael rose to continue the journey, it was with a new, cheerful optimism. Rejoiced in spirit by his new companions, and refreshed by his cleansing tears and the bracing gust of autumn that blew so pleasantly in his face, the weary trek took on a more wholesome character. Sparrow had but a small share of Dael's joy, but she was happy too. She would think of Rydl no more, she decided. She belonged to Dael now, like those pets of his.

They had not gone far when Sparrow decided to stop. There was something she needed to know, and folding her arms, she stood stubbornly in the open plain, refusing to advance. Dael had to figure out why she stopped, and what she wanted; and soon discerned what was bothering her. In an exaggerated manner Sparrow was looking with wide eyes in all directions, turning her palms upward in question. She was inquiring where they were going, and made it clear in her silent way that she would go no further until she knew. Dael debated in his mind whether he should strike her into motion, but he restrained himself. He had inwardly vowed to be patient with her.

And where *was* he going? It was but vague in his mind. When he departed from the Beautiful Country, he had informed his family that he would seek out the crimson people; but it had never been his settled intention. He had no destination. It occurred to him along the way that he might visit his deceased wife's burial place in the cave-pocked region where he was born, and where he had lived until the wasp people took him captive. After Zan rescued him (yes, he could finally acknowledge that Zan had saved him at great personal risk), Dael had returned to his home and eventually married. Why did Lissa die when their happiness together had hardly begun? It would do no good to visit her grave. That was a great distance away, far beyond the great abyss that he and Sparrow were only gradually approaching. To see her grave would only make him miserable.

"We are going to the land of red rocks, where the crimson people live," he replied to the question she had been unable to ask. "I want to become a red person." Sparrow looked askance at him, but could not ask why he wanted to live among a foreign people who painted themselves red. Dael offered no explanation because there was none. They and his people, the Ba-Coro, were not on friendly terms, and it would be risky to approach them. The only reason that Dael would seek out the red people was that they were so very different from his own. They were an alien clan—but wasn't Dael as alien as they? And didn't that make them strangely akin? Dael was drawn to the red people by invisible sinews, and Sparrow hesitantly followed.

From the Beautiful Country to the land of red rocks is a march of several days. The trajectory is downward, but unevenly so, and increasingly rough for some distance. From a high vantage point it is a many-colored journey— black turning to green, green to yellow and then to red, where the towers of stone are faintly visible. It is all seen in streaks of color fading one into another to the farthest distance. At the moment, the two sojourners were approaching a field of parching grasses tall enough to hide in and sleep on in relative safety. Unfortunately, the many grassy species produced burrs and thistles, and leaves or stems that were rough, and sharp enough to cut. It was a difficult passage, eventually relieved by a clearing where they rested.

Amid the tangle of prairie grasses now surrounding them, and peppered with dry little flowers, there were multitudes of living things small and large which were disturbed and brought to life by the march of the travelers. Dara and Nata, ambling along at an animal's leisurely pace, suddenly bounded after a hare. The wiry creature sped erratically away, fanged jaws snatching at either side. It had a moment's respite when it reached the taller grass and brambles, but the wolves soon picked up the trail and finally caught the unlucky creature. Dara, the larger of the two wolves, held it still living in her mouth, but by the time she brought it to Dael, it was as good as dead.

The animals were proud of their kill, and wanted their master to see what they had accomplished, but withdrew with their prey when Dael reached for it. Clearly Dara had mixed feelings about giving it up. Meanwhile Sparrow was watching to see what would happen, wishfully eyeing the prize. Dael had a meaty bone left in his bag, the remains of a haunch, and used it to distract his pets. When Dael tossed it into the brambles, both of them flew after it, Dara dropping the rabbit and Dael quickly taking it up. When the animals returned, with Nata holding the bone in her slobbery jaws, Dael had already begun skinning their hare. Its insides, minus the liver that Sparrow wanted, were all the hunters got, and the carcass was soon roasting on a fire.

Since his departure, Dael had been severely depressed and had very little desire to eat; but his appetite was returning with his rising spirits. The savory odor of roasting meat also had its effect. After Dael and Sparrow had consumed what they wanted, and had put something away for the next day, they tossed the bones to Dara and Nata, along with some flesh. Their animals had to eat too, and after all, the rabbit was really theirs. Sparrow had been much more hungry than Dael, and now, her stomach satisfied, she nestled between Dael and Nata, which required the wolf to make some room. She cuddled against Dael, and he put one arm around her in spite of himself, and the other around Dara. He was happy for the moment, but it was still light, and they had to move on.

As dusk approached, they luckily found an island of softer grass within the tall, rough growth. The sun was already dropping behind the mountains to the west, and the sky, gorgeously glowing, tinted the numberless bright specks of flowers with delicious hues. The travelers made themselves comfortable, while their lively companions, little inclined to rest, went foraging this way and that. It was getting late and it was time to camp. They built another fire and made a bed on the fragrant field, which provided a spot of relief from the surrounding tangle. The area was alive with murmuring insects and with tall, weedy grasses, thistles, and occasional florets spreading their profusion of miniscule wild seeds.

By the time Dael and Sparrow were settled, it was dark. Dara and Nata could still be heard playing and thrashing somewhere in the brush. An almost full moon gleamed, now bright, now dim or disappeared, momentarily obscured by passing clouds. That night, under the doubtful orb, on a soft and yielding place encircled by thorny growth, Sparrow conceived a child— while the two wolves wailed at the shadowy lantern.

3 RED ROCKS

Plants are like people; they grow where they find nourishment. The nourishment stopped quite suddenly and there was no more grassland for a long time—only scraggly bushes with stunted and twisted trunks that appeared to be struggling for life. Animals there were—goats or antelope of a kind neither Dael nor Sparrow had ever seen—but they were wary and kept well out of a hunter's range. There was so little water that it seemed remarkable anything could live or grow, but once in a while the travelers would find a pond where water had collected during the infrequent rains. It tasted brackish, but it was all they had. The region was subject to rare downpours that might swell the dried ravines and refresh the famished growth. The parched riverbeds would briefly flood, and then go down, only to swell again with the next rain.

Dael and Sparrow came across a reddish creek, which they traced for a half-day. It led them to something almost startling in this arid region—an isolated woodland, flooded and completely dead. What was it doing in this almost treeless land? It grew in a low-lying area near the stream, and it evidently had died, not from a shortage of water, but an excess that the vicinity was generally denied. In an unusually rainy year, the stream had overflowed into the basin, creating a small lake, and the trees had been drowned.

Certain species, standing in water even for a single season, will die. When the swollen river feeding them had gone down, the forest was left standing in stagnant water. Now the lifeless trees cast eerie, black branches against the sky; and the tall trunks, which had long since lost their bark and were darkened with time, were extended in length by their reflections in the stagnant pool. They had once been vital living things.

The impression this dead forest and putrid water made was so dreary, mysterious, and unexpected that the travelers felt vaguely uneasy. Even the wolves, approaching the water, sniffed as at a dead animal that repels rather than attracts. Dael and Sparrow were reluctant to drink it, and were about to change their course when their attention was further arrested by another peculiar discovery: Many of the upper branches were thickly populated by large, black birds— fit inhabitants of the mournful setting—which were doubled in number by their reflections in the gray water. They began to croak and caw woefully together, so that the entire dismal wood echoed. The alarmed birds, unused to company in that lonely spot, flew away in a dark mass, settling in a more distant area and continuing their raucous cries. Then, by common agreement, they flew as a unit still farther away, their outcries gradually diminishing as the distance increased.

Except for bees and ants, these birds appeared to be the only social creatures in the region. There had not been a single human visible on the entire long hike. In fact, the land hardly seemed hospitable to human life at all, but perhaps that was because it was so devoid of it. Dael, Sparrow, and the two wolves followed the ebony birds into the distance with their eyes, as the broad, black wings beat the autumn air.

▼ ▼ ▼

The land of red rocks, which the travelers at length reached, is entered from the west through a stone archway that partially spans an empty vale. Time and accident have eaten the arched passage through a jutting wall of rock. Under this arch stands the funeral barrow of Aniah. Dael recognized it, and now had no doubt about their position in the rocky wilderness. The great leader who lay under the barrow had died very near this spot, when the Ba-Coro were migrating in the opposite direction toward the Beautiful Country—which Aniah had not lived to enter. They had built this tower of stone over Aniah's wasted remains in his honor.

It was Aniah who had given Dael's twin his name of honor, Zan-Gah, when Zan had brought down the enemy lion. The old man had been Zan's friend—and Dael's too. Dael recalled how, when he was alive, Aniah had placed a fatherly hand on his tattooed shoulder and spoken friendly warnings at a time that he, Dael, had been so full of hatred that he could not profit from wise words. Now he wondered what could have prevented him from understanding the simple truths that Aniah had given him, or the real friendship he had offered.

On either side of the vale are high cliffs pocketed with caves and dugouts. Once one has advanced any distance, one becomes aware that there is no exit on either side, and that the only options are either to go forward or retreat. If anyone could see the four intruders walking between the high-rising cliffs, they would seem small and insignificant beside the natural grandeur of the land. Everything is red—the rocks, the walls of stone, the dusty dirt, and even the water, swelling after one of those brief, violent downpours, runs blood red. It stands alone as perhaps the reddest region in the wide world. When the setting sun falls slanting on it, the rich ground almost flames. Boulders are everywhere, scattered like giant playthings, and as their number increases they get in the way, making forward movement difficult, so that the traveler is tempted to walk from rock to rock. But before much distance is passed, the boulders are replaced by high towers of stone, often of fantastic shapes, standing like giants over the miniscule travelers.

One can rest in the shadow of these huge boulders, which is what Dael and his companions did until the descending sun tinted the land with a hallucinatory glow. But when it started to get cold, they wished they could sit in the afternoon light again. They would have to find shelter. In the distance, Dael had already made out the shape of the skull. Sparrow was frightened when

Dael pointed it out to her, but he explained that it was just a collection of pits and dugouts. He told her how he, Zan, Rydl, and some others had taken shelter in the very pit that formed the mouth of the skull. They went there now, climbing a long-established stairway of rocks and footholds, Dara and Nata scrambling after them. Dael had completely forgotten how the shape of death had inspired his lust for blood and vengeance against the wasp people. But he thought of Hurnoa. She had not been visiting his dreams as much lately.

When they arrived at the cave-like hollow, they built a fire on the cold, grayish ashes of an older one—Rydl's blaze when he had lived there, now long extinct. The wolves stood guard while they slept. Dael dreamt of Hurnoa yet again, and Sparrow of Rydl, so strangely transformed that she hardly knew him.

▼ ▼ ▼

Soon after the travelers awoke they observed that Dara and Nata were whining and restive, possibly having seen an animal and longing to hunt it down. Maybe they would bring back whatever they caught, as before. Water and food had to be found, and the four went out together to see what they could garner. Dael, spear in hand and flanked by his sniffing wolves, presented a commanding figure if there could be any to see him in this apparently empty land. Dael looked this way and that at the barren, rocky landscape. No one could live here long among these boulders and impassible cliffs, he thought. Even if they had spotted game in this maze, they could hardly have run it down; it would easily escape them. The wolves had a better chance to catch something.

Their animal companions were in fact acting strangely, meandering among the stones. Dara began to snarl, and suddenly lunged at a boulder—which promptly rose to take the form of an almost naked man! The man ran terrified from the wolf, which pursued him, snapping at his calf. He was as red as the scattered rocks and earth around him, and apparently painted with that very substance. Crouched down with his back upward, he had been easily mistaken for a boulder, and as such was as invisible as a man can be who is in fact in plain sight— although the sharper senses of the wolves had quickly detected him.

What was also completely unexpected was the sound of laughter all around them; and only when several of the boulders rose and took human forms did it become evident that the two were completely surrounded by dozens of crimson people. Sparrow scanned her captors with the look of a frightened animal, but her fears were unnecessary for the moment and quickly passed.

Clearly, although for no clear reason, these crimson people were in a cheerful mood. The sound not only of laughter but high hilarity was greeting the visitors' ears. The erstwhile boulders simply roared with cackling amusement. Was it the ease with which they had surrounded the newcomers, and the surprise registered on their faces? Undoubtedly they were enjoying the success of their camouflage. But the red men seemed to be pointing to the unusual garment of the pair, and even more to their uncolored skin—for every one of their number, men, women, and children, were painted the same crimson hue. They were not used to unpainted people, and found them curious and very funny. Little children pointed at the two, shrieking with amusement and squeezing their parents' hands in excitement.

This crimson troop carried no arms, but they were so numerous that resistance seemed useless; and luckily, resistance was unnecessary, for it quickly could be seen that these painted people intended no harm. They did not fear danger from a pair of travelers, and the presence of the spearman's woman made it clear that war was not their purpose. They seemed to like visitors, for their movements and frequent friendly touches conveyed salutation and welcome.

It took a while for Dael and Sparrow to realize that the crimson people were talking to them. Dael had heard three different languages in his lifetime, and spoke two of them, but this new one was not at all like the others. It was largely formed of a multitude of clicking, clucking, hissing, and tongue-cracking noises, unlike any language he or Sparrow had ever heard. But whatever its peculiar nature, the valley was filled at that moment with their crickets' clatter mixing with the more familiar laughter. Neither newcomer was able to make reply, but at last Sparrow flashed her broad smile, and several of the women responded, showing their ivory teeth.

The large group gathering around the strangers started walking, taking Dael and Sparrow with them in a hospitable manner, clicking and clacking the whole time. They made their way through the many rocks with the ease of familiarity, while Dael and Sparrow struggled to keep up. The wolves, which had lost interest in these people as soon as they were acquainted with them, remained close to Dael.

Flanked by these animals, and with his natural intrepidity and strength, Dael immediately gained the respect of the group. On the whole, they were not very large people, while Dael was lean, muscular, and comparatively tall. The crimson people had no pets, let alone such wild and dangerous ones, so that the company of Dara and Nata gave Dael an unusual and marked significance. Dael's rich scarifications, swirling in energetic designs over his entire body, endowed him in their minds with an almost mystical status.

4 THE CHLDREN OF THE EARTH

The crimson people resided in a large, orderly village formed of rude sod huts that were arranged in concentric circles. A huge orange rock sheltered the village from the worst of the sun. Those who lived closest to the center were the most important people of the clan, and everybody seemed to understand just where they and their family ought to live and were quite satisfied with their station. Dael, who had grown up in a dank cave along with his twin brother, was deeply impressed with the symmetry of the village; and Sparrow thought she had never seen anything so pretty. The interiors of the dwellings were dug into the red earth, so that the walls were at least half under ground, making them cooler in the summer and easier to warm in the winter. The roofs were of matted grasses. Children were always peeping or running in and out of the small, round doorways like so many crimson prairie dogs, chattering gleefully in their strange language. Their parents seemed a happy and almost carefree people.

They proved to be good hunters of many species, particularly the antelope that lived in large numbers throughout the area. Many ingenious methods of trapping them had been developed, and often the animals' speed and agility could be used against them. The crimson men would drive the fleet creatures into nets or off heights, sometimes catching quarry in whole herds against stone cliffs or rivers. There were also deer, rabbits, and swine, among other game animals. Gatherers also could find edible roots and seeds in great variety, so the inhabitants ate well both of meat and plants.

Dael had encountered these red men before, and now wondered why his people, the Ba-Coro, had been attacked by them when they were migrating to the Beautiful Country. It had been a brief skirmish, but the painted warriors, rising from the ground like boulders come to life, had drawn blood and sustained casualties. The reasons for that attack remained uncertain in Dael's mind, but the presence of dozens of armed warriors passing through their country might well have looked like an invasion to the residents.

The reception of Dael and Sparrow was very different, because a lone traveling pair posed no danger. No one seemed to remember Dael's role in the earlier fight, which had been fatal to two; and Dael saw no reason to remind his new hosts of that brief but bloody encounter— especially since they now were treating the newcomers so kindly. With his bitter experience of captivity behind him, and his ingrained combative tendencies, Dael little expected to be generously welcomed by a stranger people, and perhaps might have been as comfortable with harshness. He could understand nothing of the tongue-clicking chatter with which he was surrounded, and was unaware of the strong impression he had made.

Particularly, his wolves drew wary stares and comments, since the crimson people had no knowledge of tame animals. Indeed, to see Dael was to fear him, covered as he was with carved designs, and flanked by beasts clearly under his command. He had been in their presence only moments before someone noticed that he was left-handed—a wonder to them—and it was quietly said that Dael might wield a new, unaccustomed power. So even before he had reached the village he enjoyed a certain prestige. He and Sparrow were placed in an abandoned hut well within the outskirts of the circle—but only after being introduced to a crimson-painted chieftain whose redness was augmented by a lavish garment of red feathers that hung to his toes.

Dael was schooling himself in patience. Seared by experience to a knowledge of the world and himself, he awaited events with no hint of his habitual ferocity. Formerly so certain that any path on which he set his foot was the right one, he was forced by the traumas he had sustained to reexamine things that once he was very sure of. Only lately he had hardly known where he was going, and he still did not know why he continued on. What did it matter where he lived, or if he lived at all? Positioned, therefore, between fierce energy and utter indifference, Dael became quiet and passive.

Meanwhile, Sparrow was making friends. Used to being unable to speak, her lack of knowledge of the language presented hardly more difficulty here than her impairment had at home. And strange to say, she would soon begin to make some of the same clicking noises and inflections as her new acquaintances. Completely dumb to the Ba-Coro, she would speedily learn a few of the new percussive words, as if her long-captive tongue had suddenly been freed. What baffled her in one language was surprisingly accessible in another. These sounds used entirely different parts of her mouth and throat than those that Rydl had touched. They called upon completely different breathing and muscles where she had never developed the disabling inhibitions that had prevented her from speaking her own language.

It was not long before Sparrow realized that the drums and hollow logs frequently rattling in the village were also speaking the language she was learning. How remarkable that drums could actually utter, and in fact shout, their messages across the plain! Unfortunately for Dael, none of this was available to him without the greatest difficulty and severest limitation. He was not naturally a sociable person, as Sparrow was, and learning a new tongue did not come easily, although after several months he would be able to make his needs known. Sparrow, on the other hand, was speedily shedding her shyness and would become a veritable chatterbox. She could soon talk to the women by the hour as she joined them in their chores, and played games with the crimson children, so that their chirping voices would mix into a happy noise, full of clicks, lip-pursing sounds, and shrieking laughter. And Sparrow would be, for some time, as necessary to Dael as to a little child because she soon could communicate and he could not. Never before had Sparrow felt so loved and accepted. Her new friends practically adopted her when they discovered that she was pregnant; and they would twinkle smiles at Dael and look at him from the corners of their eyes.

It was Dael who first painted his body red, an example Sparrow quickly followed. Nobody had suggested it because their hosts correctly guessed that they would adapt to the customs in time without being urged. They were in that and in many respects a polite and gentle people. Soon enough their crimson color seemed quite natural, and the absence of paint looked like a form of nakedness. Indeed, Sparrow was not used to so much nudity, but no one appeared to feel exposed or troubled, so neither was she. During the warm season, coloring was their principal clothing. Every part of the body was reddened but the soles of their feet, which reddened themselves as they walked on the deep-dyed ground.

Dael's tattoos almost disappeared under the earthen application that more than anything else helped to make him a true member of the tribe. Sparrow almost laughed at the change. But the brilliantly hued skin, which looked so very odd at first, became almost invisible after a while, and only its absence seemed notable or strange. As Sparrow's time approached, her swollen belly resembled a great crimson melon. Her healthy face took on a dreamy look quite outside of herself, while a tiny new being kicked from within.

The red men were not a warlike people, only jealous of their unique crimson land. The ground was sacred to them, and they called themselves the Children of the

Earth. The act of painting themselves with the flaming natural pigment bound them to the earth and made them part of it. It was their Mother, and they were its children. Almost all of their rituals served to augment this relationship, and to bind them to each other as brothers and sisters. To be called "earth-born" was the highest of compliments.

Dael, whose whole life involved war and conflict, was genuinely surprised to learn how peaceable these people were. They gave little thought to battle, which they regarded as an unpleasant waste of resources, and in fact had small inclination to compete with each other over anything. Cooperation and sharing were their rules of life; they always seemed to be building something of red stone or red earth, engaged together like a community of eager insects dedicated to a communal purpose. Dael was fascinated by their constructive vigor at a time when his own level of energy was at low ebb. The rocks once were people, they told him, but the gods, tired of their noisy quarrels and wars, had transformed them for their misbehavior.

Not that the Children of the Earth lacked weapons. One in particular intrigued Dael when he finally understood what it was. It consisted of a flexible rod bent at both ends by a connecting string of hide or sinew. Its purpose was to fling small, sharp spears, and it was both accurate and deadly. They called it something that in their language meant bow and arrow. The red men used it exclusively for hunting, and would hardly have dreamed of employing it against humans—except in the extreme case of a gross and impious invasion of their red earth-mother, which no one seemed to anticipate, but probably would have resisted to the last member of the tribe.

As Dael slowly learned the language of his hosts (with much help from Sparrow), he was able to ask about the many things that puzzled him. What greatly surprised him was that the red men had no intention of using their deadly weapons in war and conquest. In vain he tried to understand their want of ambition. They just built or hunted, hunted or built, raised their children, and engaged in their rituals—and had no thought of warfare. Surely these painted people were backward, Dael considered to himself. But the more he reflected, the more he had to wonder whether it was he and the Ba-Coro who were backward, at least in many respects, and not the red men. How would his father and his huge, ungainly uncle, Chul, fare in this setting? Dael almost smiled to think of Chul painted red.

There were a number of ritual practices that Dael and Sparrow had never seen and found exceedingly odd. Sparrow was more quickly accepting of them than Dael, who was mystified and perplexed. There were solemn acrobatic games, handling of poisonous snakes, and other magic practices, sometimes led by the spirit-man. When the sun descended in the evening, setting the sky afire with orange and rose, the men spoke to the glowing sphere with thundering drums, imploring it to return in the morning. At these times of worship, the red earth itself became more luminous and crimson, and every person faced the same direction in reverent silence until it slowly grew dark and the flaming brilliance was gone. Then the drums would suddenly cease.

Among the women, the moon became the focus of their devotions, particularly when it was full, and low in the sky. At that hour, it seemed unusually large and took on a sultry copper glow. They would retell the story of the moon's marriage to the brightest of stars, in a ceremony attended by all the other stars in the sky. Then female musicians would serenade the orb with their wooden flutes, making a sweet, cooing sound that contrasted greatly with the rattling commotion of the drums. What an eerie thing it was, yet beautiful too, to hear the strange melodies hailing the moon with soft, worshipful messages! But soon, as their ritual drink strongly affected them, the thundering drums would speak again and for a time their music became a kind of madness.

Of all the many curious customs of his adopted people, what Dael found hardest to accept was that the women of the tribe governed. It was true, he discovered to his horror! The rituals were directed mainly by women, and all major decisions were made by them—although their spirit-man would be consulted occasionally. But rarely did they include their husbands in any meaningful way. Maybe that was why the crimson people exhibited so little manly aggression, Dael judged.

Their council of elders consisted entirely of females, and was headed by a great plump matron named Mlaka (as nearly as Dael could approximate it in his own language). A widow, she had four sons who helped her rule the men, all minor chieftains of sorts, while her two daughters did almost nothing. Mlaka, who lived in the center of the circular village, was protected, served, and adored by everyone—like the queen bee at the heart of a great red hive.

Dael never once saw Mlaka for a whole year. She stayed inside her large, five-sided dwelling, and was attended exclusively by other women. Sparrow was brought to her presence soon after their arrival, and instructions were given for the reception of the stranger couple. Then neither Sparrow nor Dael saw her any more for a long time.

5 HEALING POWER

There is a healing power in kindness, and Dael began to mend. His adopted clan asked nothing of him or Sparrow. The mild painted people gave them a place to live and shared food with them, so that all their needs were met. At every turn the newcomers received kindness and friendship—which sometimes is more important than mere material generosity.

Sparrow accepted it all easily because she was of a like generous disposition and was just as quick to befriend and share with others; but Dael was at first as puzzled and perplexed as if he had been badly received or even cruelly treated. Who knows what harshness he had expected at their hands? If it was penance he sought here, he tasted a different kind of correction than he had anticipated, and was taught some new, simple lessons quite removed from his expectations. In time Dael came to accept the natural warmth of the red people, and return it in some measure. Sometimes, indeed, the corners of his mouth turned upward, and he even smiled at his round-bellied woman when she was chattering so happily with other women of the tribe. Then he thought of Lissa-Na and became sad again.

Dael still was afflicted by horrific nightmares. It did not matter what the dream was about—his childhood, his mother, Lissa, his twin, or the fruit of a tree—Hurnoa's dreadful apparition would drive them away or cause them to wither. Anything he loved or felt at peace with would flee from her ghastly image like a frightened spirit in the presence of a powerful, malignant magician. He never dreamed of his torturers any more—only of her.

Dael's nocturnal disturbances were noticed in the village. One time a neighbor who heard a loud scream inquired if he was in pain. That was when Dael first met Koli. Kho-Kholi was his name, but "Koli" was the closest Dael could get to pronouncing it, once they became friends. On that first occasion Sparrow shunted the alarmed visitor away, assuring him that Dael would be all right; but the next morning Koli inquired again about the ghosts that were troubling Dael, talked to him a little, and advised him to visit the spirit-man. By then Dael had recovered and quietly said that he would consider Koli's advice. Koli was already convinced that Dael was on special terms with the world of spirits—an impression that was gaining credence in other quarters as well.

Dael's reputation as a man of special faculties, arising the first day he had been in the company of the red men, was increasing. His power became an object of conversation one day when he needed to make a fire. Fire was easily available to him, for it was a mark of hospitality and friendship among the red men to share it. The painted people only knew how to make fire by striking certain rocks together to make sparks—which was a difficult and laborious process. Someone always had a blaze going, however, and no one would ever fail to share a burning twig. Indeed, these generous people were used to sharing almost everything. But Dael still had trouble communicating and was reluctant to ask favors, so he took out his fire-making instrument, which produced fire by friction. The sage elder, Aniah, had given this secret tool to Zan, and Dael had learned how to make one for himself.

When Dael had arranged the thong with which the kindling heat was generated, and laid out the dry tinder in the sunlight, a curious crowd was already gathering. A wisp of rising smoke wafted toward their noses, and when the tinder burst into flame, a buzz of amazement stirred. The stranger's magic was marveled at, and news of it spread throughout the village like another fire. People talked of it for weeks, but curiously no one was inclined to try the magic or adopt it for himself. The red people continued to make and share fire as they always had done. But Dael's status as a special person was established.

Dael's mystique was enlarged by another activity involving fire. It might well have been supposed that anything Dael cooked over his amazing blaze might prove in some way peculiar and surprising, and it turned out to be so: Dael's deceased wife, Lissa-Na, who had been of a distant people, the Noi, was skilled and knowledgeable in the use of herbs—for flavoring, preservatives, and medicine. Dael, full of admiration, had learned some of her skill. Now, many were puzzled to see him rubbing some fragrant leaves onto a roast to make it savory, and were pleasantly surprised by the odor. Since some friends had given the meat to Sparrow, she decided to invite them to partake. There was a delighted uproar, which soon was conveyed around the village. Never did a joint of meat disappear so quickly! Sparrow explained that the aromatic herb was very common in the area, and this time the discovery was not ignored. Soon, no haunch was roasted without it, and the sweet smell was almost always in the air.

Lissa-Na had also taught Dael some of her healing arts. Special leaves, berries, and roots were known to her healing order, and Dael learned about some few of them from her. Whether Dael's preparations cured a sick child, or the child had simply recovered naturally, Dael was suddenly credited with knowledge of a wonderful magic; and a mixture that took the sting from wounds most certainly worked, so that several tribesmen called on him for help, and spread his fame. Dael also retained knowledge of the wasp men's poison, but he kept that secret to himself.

News of the skills Dael employed came to the ears of the clan's spirit-man, who was disturbed to learn that he had a rival in the use of magic substances. Among the males, Shnur was surely the most powerful and respected of the red people—and feared. He had no intention of sharing his position with a newcomer, and began to watch Dael more closely, for he had already heard much about him.

6 KOLI

It was not the first time that Dael had anticipated being a father. The loss of his wife and baby had been so deep a wound that he had never completely recovered; and now, as Dael looked at Sparrow's increasing fullness, he dreaded that the same thing would happen again. Not that Sparrow could ever replace Lissa-Na, but she and the coming baby were his life now whether he liked it or not.

And on balance he did like it. Sparrow was an entirely different person since she had come to this red place, learning to speak for the first time in her life, and shedding her inhibiting shyness. It would it not be an exaggeration to say that Dael was a different person too. He had gradually forgotten all thoughts of conflict and vengeance, and his bad dreams became less frequent for a while. He was engaging with a few friends, and eagerly looking forward to fatherhood. Dael cared for his pregnant woman through the winter, as though she and her burden were too precious to neglect—his greatest fear being that Sparrow would die in childbirth and the baby along with her. For her sake he became very watchful and attentive. Sparrow was not used to such treatment, and began to look at Dael in a new way.

When Sparrow's time came the next summer, she was assisted in her labor by the matron's daughters. It was their only function. Sparrow had become friends with both of them, and was grateful for their help; although she quietly wished that her own mother could be there. She had a fairly easy delivery, with the additional help of the spirit-man, Shnur, whose dancing antics so frightened her as to speed up the processes of birth. Dael was presented with a fine son, to his delight, and from that point forward a series of broad hints from almost everyone he encountered urged him to wed the mother of his child, according to their custom.

Among the numerous acquaintances that encouraged him to the ceremony, the foremost was Koli, who, in his joking way, presented all the advantages of marriage: "You will truly be one of us," he said. "All of our men marry the first chance they get, and with the very first woman they meet, excepting their mothers and sisters! I don't jest about these matters, ha ha ha! And won't you look fine wearing white stripes!" he declared, laughing heartily without explaining his words. He neglected to mention that he himself was single.

Dael was fortunate in this friendship. He was little inclined to seek the company of anyone himself, but Koli had repeatedly sought him out, inviting him to join in the hunt and in various other activities. Koli taught him the use of the bow and arrow, and helped him with the still unfamiliar language.

There are some people, and Dael was one, who exhaust their energies swimming against the current of their personal river—their emotions. Others, for some reason unknown even to themselves, seem always to be speeding along with, and carried by, that same current. Koli was of this second type. He appeared never to have spent an unhappy or conflicted day in his life. Everybody seemed to like him, and he liked everybody, was confident of good luck, and greatly enjoyed a joke. He could fill the air with his boisterous laugh and manly, booming voice, which was easily recognized even from a distance.

Koli had long black hair that he did not shave (contrary to the practice of most of his tribe), and a fine set of strong white teeth. When he laughed, which was frequently, his healthy grinders would flash his good spirits, making a favorable impression that lasted long after his lips were closed. He was taller than most of his tribe, and powerfully built. Both his dark mane and his gleaming teeth contrasted emphatically with his reddened face and muscular, painted body. He was a handsome man, and a happy one. The girls were unanimously fond of Koli and were always flirting with him.

It was a peculiarity of Koli's personality that he never seemed to need much of anything, and might well have given his finest possession to the first person that asked for it. People flocked to be with him, refusing his gifts and admiring his freedom from needing things. But Koli gave much more than gifts. He cheerfully gave of himself, his happiness, and his lightness of heart. Quickly discerning that Dael was sad and of a gloomy temperament, Koli adopted him to his good humor.

He would converse and laugh with Sparrow too, as if she were the most talkative of ladies, and managed to conquer her initial shyness. Later, after her delivery, no one took more delight in bouncing and playing with the new baby than he.

This merry comrade was as an antidote to Dael's gloom. His lighthearted buoyancy of spirit strongly contrasted to Dael's grave and cheerless disposition, and the exchange between them served to brighten Dael's mood. Good-natured, optimistic, athletic, irresistible, Koli was always joyous, always sure that game was at hand—and so he cheered the hunt.

Dael, who had been used to being the leader in his life with the Ba-Coro, was content to be a follower now—Koli's "little brother." Here was a companion Dael could look up to in his sour way. There had been his uncle, Chul, of course, but Chul, though strong, could be a great oaf, and Dael had never liked him. Koli was the only person who could make Dael laugh; and from him Dael was slowly relearning how to enjoy life.

Koli had one grievous fault: he had an unfortunate compulsion to play tricks on his friends. Not that he actually kept the roast he snatched while the neighbor cook's back was turned. He put it in its place again as soon as the outraged victim was gone to look for it. How Koli bellowed with laughter! Strong as a bull, he would place heavy boulders in doorways and play innocent, but his noisy laughter gave him away. He loved to wrestle and play with Dael's wolves, and would tease them with food or tie things to their tails—until Dael made him stop. He would tickle Sparrow's neck with a straw and tell her that there was a beetle on it—but by that time she could not be fooled, and gave him a good-natured scolding.

Dael joined in the fun and started playing tricks too: Suddenly, Sparrow's new baby was missing! Sparrow, of course, knew exactly where it was, and went directly to Koli's hut to reclaim it. And there it was—but when she would go out with the recovered infant, the door was blocked by an enormous rock. Koli exploded with laughter. "Babies are good bait," he roared, "if you want to capture the mother!" Then it was Dael's turn to be scolded for helping.

Dael told his friend about Rydl—how Dael had disliked and pestered him. (He wondered in retrospect why.) Rydl, determined to put a stop to his persecutions, had set a trap for Dael, he recounted, and Dael stepped into the snare while hunting for his enemy. Up Dael sprang upside-down, held by his ankle to a flexible tree and left to hang there in midair. Koli roared with delight at this story, and Dael, laughing too, warned Koli that he knew how to set the same trap for him. Koli laughed even more, slapping his crimson thigh.

▼ ▼ ▼

The wedding of Dael and Sparrow was commemorated with unusual excitement. Ritual drinking and the appeal of drums and flutes to the goddess of the earth produced an unwonted wildness; for they were not only celebrating the marriage, and recognizing the birth of a child, but welcoming three new members to their clan—

strangers who were adopting their customs and ways. The ritual bound them to the tribe and to the sacred earth as much as to each other.

In preparation for the ceremony, the bodies of Dael and Sparrow were decorated with a rare white pigment that contrasted against their crimson skin. Ten fingers dipped in white paint were artistically drawn across their limbs, torsos, and faces, making parallel stripes in sets of five. Finger-painted zigzag patterns of remarkable intricacy embellished Dael from head to toe; and Sparrow was similarly decorated in elaborate curvilinears and spirals. Xiti, their new baby who had been given a name familiar to their adopted people, was likewise decorated in the angular zigzag patterns of a male. Xiti was passed from hand to hand by adoring friends, and became almost the central figure, while Dael and Sparrow were hailed as if they had accomplished a wonderful feat.

In true fact, their marriage had relieved considerable anxiety among their crimson friends, for begetting children without the due ceremony of a wedding was unheard of among them and seriously frowned upon. Only their alien status, and the natural reticence of an innately polite people, had saved Dael and Sparrow from censure. Nobody had known of their unmarried state at first, but Sparrow, now a talker, told all.

The following day, Koli visited the newlyweds, bringing bright, beaded gifts and congratulating them with his characteristic booming voice. But as soon as he had a chance, he pulled Dael aside with a whisper and a grave expression that was far from typical of him. One look at Koli convinced Dael that something was wrong, and he immediately asked what the matter was.

"Have you done something to offend Shnur?" Koli asked.

"Who?"

"Shnur, the spirit-man."

"No, I don't think so. Has he said anything?"

"I saw him last night giving you very unpleasant looks—you know how his eyes bulge when he is angry—and he was mumbling something that might have been curses or magic. What can you have done to offend him? There was hatred in his glance, I am sure!"

"I don't know," Dael replied. "I can't imagine what it might be."

"Shnur is a powerful and dangerous man, Dael. Beware of him! I foresee trouble!"

Dael made no reply, but searched his memory for any event that might have provoked Shnur's enmity.

7 SHNUR'S ENMITY

The spirit-man was one of those unlucky people who always can find fault with a friend, who can detect an insult where none is intended, and see a supposed new danger well beyond the farthest horizon. His very glance was baleful. Older than most, gaunt and wiry in figure, his bony skull sat like a carbuncled knob on top of his sinewy neck. Long, unruly hair jutted from his head in spikes, giving him a jagged silhouette from any angle; while his yellowed eyes, red-veined, added to his ferocious appearance—which he did not wish to conceal.

He was frightening to look at, even without the accouterments of his trade; and on this fear he generally relied, for the power of his magic stemmed from it. He could convince a strong man that his death was imminent, and that man, however healthy, was very apt to die of the morbid expectation. It once actually happened thus to one of his critics, and the whole village took notice. Shnur's frightened victim, ever looking over his shoulder in anticipation of disaster, paled, sickened, and eventually died as foretold.

Shnur healed in much the same way, persuading the afflicted that his magical skills and the right gifts could go far toward making them well. His magic worked because there is no sorcery so effective as the one that people believe in. And people did believe.

Shnur was the shaman of the crimson people. Whether by art or accident, his reputation for healing and magic had grown over the thirty years since he had become a man. It was generally believed that no misfortune or sickness befell anybody but through the action of wicked spirits; and Shnur had convinced his people and himself that he could communicate with these spirits and influence their behavior. He was known as a mediator who could persuade unfriendly ghosts by giving them presents and bribes—although he also could flatter them or threaten them into compliance. Shnur could go into trances and wrestle with the troublesome spirits too, but he said that it was dangerous, and expected to be paid for his services. The matrons of the clan sometimes came to him with community problems, and he would enter into the supernatural world to find their solutions. If anyone was disturbed by a dream, Shnur could tell him just what it meant; but for this, too, he expected to be paid. It was whispered that he could control the future.

Shnur lived in one of the largest, and certainly the most elaborately decorated of the houses, and was often seen sitting rigidly in front of it on his spindly crossed legs. He would look straight ahead with piercing eyes, speaking to no one, and no one daring to speak to him. During these periods of rigid quiescence, he would react to nothing around him, although sometimes he could be heard mumbling to gods or spirits. He could sit thus for whole days—but he might begin twitching violently, suddenly leaping up and screaming something to the sun, and falling down in a fit. His startled and awestruck audience would form a ring around him while he writhed, waiting for him to rise and possibly make a mystic pronouncement, or even sing a riddling song in his raspy voice. Then scratching himself, he would retire to his hut without another word.

Most of the time Shnur seemed calm and dignified, however, and little given to emotional display; but in reality his heart was full of venomous passions which he was always on guard to conceal—except at the times when an emotional explosion could seem to augment his magic. He had two wives and five children who were expected to be silent in his presence. All of them appeared to hate him—although hostility was not commonly displayed in front of the gentle crimson people.

Among his tribe he was more feared than loved, but many called on him when they needed help—were sick, frightened, or troubled by bad dreams—and Shnur grew wealthy, for generous gifts of food, hides, tools, and weapons were always the price of his magic. He paid his sons to help him manage his affairs, and loved to have them line up his material possessions in neat stacks. He was the brother of Mlaka, the great matron, and enjoyed considerable prestige from that connection.

Shnur was jealous of his position and defensive about his powers. He instantly detested anyone who seemed to doubt them, even for a moment. He disliked several men of the tribe, especially Koli, for whom he nevertheless pretended friendship, always greeting him with a portion of a smile. But Shnur's face would shrivel like a drying grape after Koli passed, and he attempted black magic behind his back—which so far proved ineffectual.

Why Shnur should bear bad feelings toward that jovial fellow would be hard to say, and Shnur might not have been able to explain it himself; but his antipathy grew to a deep hatred in the space of about a year. A reasonless antagonism it was, for Koli had committed no offense against him, nor was any man in the village better liked—but might that not have been at least a partial cause of the magician's enmity? Why does ugliness hate beauty, and meanness despise generosity? Shnur was not a generous man, and Koli was. Why do insecure, nervous people turn against happy, positive ones? Koli's great offense was that he enjoyed life, whereas the shaman, for all his wealth and prestige, did not. Koli had that boundless confidence which is a river of energy to a happy man; while the shaman was only able to vent his hostility by covert, sneaky acts. He mumbled rather than railed, and cast fruitless spells in secret.

The spirit-man had still another reason to hate Koli: Koli's close new companion, Dael, was a man that Shnur suspected for his powers as a magician, considering him a potential rival. He had seen fewer signs of Dael's supernatural capacities than had come to his ears, but those that reached him were exaggerated out of all proportion, so that he foresaw intolerable competition for the position that had made him rich. Had he known of Dael's visits to the spirit world in his life with the Ba-Coro, and the authority Dael had once enjoyed among them, Shnur would have been still more watchful, and would have regarded this stranger as an even more immediate threat.

Koli was too confident and outgoing to be very perceptive, and it was a long time before he suspected that Shnur's overly affable looks might conceal something sinister. It was the magician's dark behavior toward Dael, which Koli observed from a distance, that first alerted him to his own danger. He reflected on Shnur's half-smiles, and suddenly he became suspicious on his own account.

Koli had little fear from the man. He understood that Shnur wielded power in the tribe, but Koli was too well liked to worry much about one cranky old adversary; and besides, he had nothing much to do with him. Koli's life was not troubled with the kind of problems that drew people to a medicine man, nor was he much inclined to mysticism and magic. As for Dael, he was not afraid of anybody living, and indeed the spirit-man had no knowledge of the potential violence and suddenness of Dael's character. Habitual caution, rather than insight, caused the shaman to watch and wait.

8 THE CROWS

Near the land of giant red rocks, where the painted people lived, there were few trees. There was, however, one that burst upward through a split boulder—which seemed sufficiently painful both to tree and rock. Planted perhaps by a bird or chipmunk ages earlier, every additional year it pushed the two sections farther apart with seemingly the greatest difficulty and the most stubborn resistance. Possibly it had been growing there since the red dwellers first began coloring their bodies— instructed by a revered ancestor on the art and virtue of camouflage. This tree, large though it was, was a sickly thing—singed by lightning numerous times, blasted, diseased, twisted, tortured, and sad. One might have thought, looking at it, that it was the sorriest specimen since the sprouting of the first tree. Yet, stripped and miserable as it was, it was the home of thousands of living creatures small and large. For on its charred and broken body lived innumerable insects, songbirds, small mammals and scurrying reptiles, so that the dying trunk and branches hosted a teeming array of animal life.

To cap off its apparent desolation, the upper branches were thick-implanted with a legion of large, coal-black crows that sat on its heights like dark, unreachable fruit. This was close to the village. Crows like to be around people for their own secret reasons, although people do not generally enjoy the presence of the crows. They are noisy, raucous creatures when the least bit disturbed, and their hoarse voices are not pleasant to human ears. The dark birds perched aloft for long periods, except when they would suddenly fly off by mutual agreement (they did almost everything as a group), in order to scour the land for food—which was anything and everything they could find. They had their leaders, and those of subordinate rank knew their places and followed where they were led.

The crows spoke their own disagreeable language, and recognized each other's individual croaking voices. Among the red earth people, theirs was considered to be a unique tongue; and it was even said that humans first learned to speak from them. So there subsisted between the two groups a kind of restrained tolerance if not amity—a red society living alongside a black one.

Dael and occasionally Sparrow, carrying their baby with them, sometimes walked in the vicinity of the sickly tree; and strange to say, the great black birds seemed to know the couple, turned to face and watch them, and made no protest of their presence. They probably remembered the two from a former acquaintance, and had no quarrel with them—although Dael soon learned that it was best to leave his wolf pets behind.

Occasionally, on these walks Dael would bring some seeds or scraps of meat, and after many tries, succeeded in tempting one of their number to descend—provided Dael placed the morsels far enough from himself to present no danger to his still suspicious new friend. The creature would move its head from one side to another in short jerky movements to best position one of its eyes on what was being offered. When it seemed safe it would hop by starts to the food, snatch it, and promptly fly away before swallowing.

It soon became Dael's daily project to visit the skittish crows, and over a period of several weeks he was able to get this single bird to venture closer and closer until at last, after many coaxing efforts, it was eating tidbits out of Dael's hand. Other birds started coming down from the treetop too, although none would come so close as the one Dael called Kraw.

The Children of the Earth, and especially Koli, were impressed and fascinated by these accomplishments, and Shnur soon enough heard all about them. Shnur wondered. He was perplexed. He pondered them so much that he could not sleep at night, and decided he had to see for himself. One day, without going too close, and hiding himself behind the large monolith that shaded the village, he observed everything. There were Dael, Koli, and baby Xiti surrounded by their ebony friends (to the joy and delight of the child) in perfect concord, sharing lunch. Dael amused himself further by hiding a morsel under a shell, but Kraw cleverly turned the shell over to retrieve it. Then Kraw suddenly flew away, and so did all the others—possibly because they had espied the intruder. Shnur saw everything, and conjectured for many days thereafter what it meant, making guesses that surely would have amazed Dael and caused Koli to roar with laughter.

Shnur considered that the invasion of the black drove's territory should have elicited a jarring chorus of angry caws, and the magician, looking on from a distance, was puzzled by Dael's success with them. Shnur, who trafficked so much with ghosts, had no difficulty in thinking of the birds as spirits too—spirits as black as night speaking insidious messages with their harsh, criminal voices *to whoever could understand them*. And Dael, who was already identified as a dangerous master of wolves, was now seen as a chieftain among the evil birds as well. Dael sometimes talked to Kraw as he fed it, and Shnur mightily wondered what he could be saying.

Dael did not think of the crows as ugly or wicked. He admired their handsome, black feathers and the blue or greenish sheen that light produced on them. The birds, among the largest he had ever seen, were sociable, talkative, and remarkably intelligent—a little bit like the clicking red people—and Dael liked them. It was calming to this once violent and troubled man to feed the friendly creatures and say a few coaxing words to them. But Shnur had always abhorred the crows. He had long been engaged in a kind of war with his dark-plumed neighbors, throwing stones at any that came close, and hissing imprecations in their direction. And the crows soon returned his hatred, for he could never approach their habitation without being visited with a cacophony of hoarse cries and flapping wings—all of which Shnur took as a personal affront.

In his angry acts of hostility Shnur had not been cautious, for, as any child of the village knew, crows have long and spiteful memories. They never forget an offense committed against a single one of them, and in fact can bear a grudge for many years. A kindly act is remembered and the friend sometimes is even followed around and visited, as was Dael's case. But crows recognize the face of an enemy, and even though Shnur sometimes wore a mask in his magic ceremonies, his face and his mask both were known and loathed by the black population. Wherever he walked, he was apt to be greeted by loud, raspy calls of alarm; and though he had only a few adversaries among the kindly crimson people, the number was greatly multiplied within the crow community.

Shnur once took it into his head to chop down the tree in which they roosted, but with a stone ax it was a difficult, noisy labor, and he was immediately attacked by swooping birds, whose sharp beaks made the project impossible to complete. After that, he was apt to be physically attacked on any occasion, as well as being screeched and cawed at; and his hatred of the black enemies reached a fever pitch. Their dark color, scolding voices, and even the reddish interior of their mouths were suspect in his mind. Shnur was sure the birds were witches, and loathed them with his heart. And that detestation he easily transferred to Dael and

Koli. The spirit-man marked the movements of the crows very closely as they flew here and there, and now he was watching Dael and Koli as well.

Neither Dael nor Koli could understand Shnur's wrath, or guess at its depth, having committed no offense against him. Eventually they recognized a hostility that the magician could scarcely conceal; but they failed to grasp its full significance, and did not foresee the unhappy consequences of it.

One afternoon, when the sun shone brightly on the red ground in front of Dael's and Sparrow's dwelling, Dael, who was keeping company with Koli, noticed a shadow pass. Looking up to see what cast it, Dael saw that Kraw had alighted on the pole that supported the roof of his small house. The bird made no sound, but eyed Dael as he walked, clearly hoping to be fed by the human it had chosen to befriend.

"Don't move, Koli," Dael whispered, and he went to get some morsels that the bird might like.

Dael immediately reappeared with pieces of dried meat in his hand. In this altered environment the crow was unwilling to approach very close at first, but Dael finally teased it into reaching into his open palm for a mouthful, while Koli with effort held his peace. Then Dael pinched another tidbit between his finger and thumb with the intention of holding onto it, so that Kraw would have to work a little to wrest it from him.

Kraw was an older crow, as one could tell by its size and disheveled feathers, some few of which were missing.

Dael didn't know if it was male or female. The skin on its feet was grayish and wrinkled, and it might have been a little sick with old age. The bird hobbled rather than walked toward his offering with a sideways step, and was about to try for the food when there was the whooshing sound of an arrow—and Dael saw that his crow had been shot. The arrow pierced through, but did not exit the unfortunate bird. Kraw flew away with the bloody shaft still in its body, and was not seen again.

The neighborhood crows could be heard screaming frantically in the distance. They always knew what was happening when their own were concerned. They stirred and swept madly overhead in large circling flights, crying their rage and discontent, and then sped away. Dael was so surprised by the arrow and the sudden flutter that he stood almost paralyzed. When he turned, he saw the grim and tight-lipped face of the magician, who, in his accumulated fury, had done the cruel mischief.

Shnur had this to learn about Dael: that he was not a man to trifle with. The magician did not realize how close to death he was, nor had he any idea of Dael's capacity for furious violence. What would Shnur have thought if he knew how ruthlessly his enemy had slain Hurnoa and indeed numerous others? Dael, who had long restrained that terrible side of his personality, was so angry that he might have killed the magician on the spot. He seized the bow out of Shnur's hand, struck him across the cheek with it, picked him up by the crotch until his feet were off the ground, and threw him down on his belly. He might have gone further had not Koli, and Sparrow who was near by, held him back.

A group of tribesmen gathered, and although both Dael and Koli were generally liked, the people could not approve of violence against their shaman, a much honored figure among them. Shnur, shaken but not badly hurt, picked himself off the ground, brushed himself, and showed his characteristic half-smile—which was prompted by the thought that his enemy had undone himself with this act. Holding his bruised cheek, he instructed some of his supporters to seize Dael and take him before the matron, Mlaka, who was the supreme judge of the Children of the Earth, and who was also his sister.

9 MLAKA'S JUSTICE

Mlaka was a huge, obese woman, five years the senior of her brother. She spent almost her entire life inside her sizable house—far the largest in the village—tended by a number of other large, plump women who catered to her every need. One would have thought that she would adopt an imperious air, having absolute authority over her village, but she was in fact kindly, motherly, good humored, and restrained. It was her job to settle disputes, but she hated conflict and rancor, and was always trying to smooth things over with the minimum of pain to anybody. Sometimes she even gave gifts to a losing party to ease the hurt of an adverse settlement. Flabby, elderly, her face puffy and not very attractive, she was yet adored by her people.

Mlaka's word was law. No one would think of gainsaying her judgments. Her relationship to the Mother, the earth, was a fundamental belief of the painted people, and disobedience to her amounted to sacrilege in their eyes.

When the red men approached her house with their strident anger, she happened to be licking some honey off her fingers. No one else in the tribe ate honey unless Mlaka personally bestowed a taste on a favorite—which she frequently did, allowing the chosen one to lick her finger. Hearing the approaching uproar, Mlaka quietly groaned to herself. What now? There never seemed to be any peace!

She signaled to one of her women to position her stool, a polished wooden stump of a seat, which was nevertheless handsomely carved with images of sun, moon, and stars. A rich, dark wood it was, that came from a long distance away. Shnur himself had fashioned the stool, for he was a skilled craftsman. Mlaka sat on it whenever there was a meeting of the matrons, an audience, or, as in this case, when she was called upon to dispense justice. It was the only chair in the village (wooden furniture being almost unknown), and rudimentary as it was, it served as a kind of throne, endowing her who sat on it with increased respect.

Dael had offered no resistance to his escort. He and the crowd, led by the bellowing magician and accompanied by Sparrow with Xiti in her arms, and Koli, who had seen everything, made their way into Mlaka's glorified shack. The woven and gabled roof made an ample space over their heads, and joints of meat and fruit hung drying from the rafters, along with a large piece of a honeycomb, which dripped a little on the earthen floor. The matron was seated on her stool, and six women flanked her, three on each side. One was fanning her.

Mlaka momentarily winced when the shaman began to speak in his furious tone. She loved her younger brother, but there was a good deal about him that made her uncomfortable; for his life was marked by fierce energy and activity, while hers was notably quiet and passive—at least she tried to make it so. Inwardly disturbed, she kept her countenance unmoved, however, and called for quiet while Shnur spoke.

In his fast-speaking way, and talking in a higher voice than usual, Shnur told her everything that had happened, omitting only his slaughter of the crow, which indeed had started all the trouble. Koli spoke up to mention that provocation, whereupon Shnur explained the necessity of killing a malicious spirit, and expanded on Dael's intimacy with the entire evil group. The whole story was told, with dark suggestions of how Dael had formed an unnatural friendship with the flock, how he had made friends with that particular crow, and how he would talk to it and the others, whose language and foul messages Dael obviously could understand. The whole time the shaman was speaking, he shook a bony finger at his enemy—a finger that was almost doubled in length by the long nail.

"Did you dare to strike my brother?" Mlaka demanded in her almost soprano voice, not without an evident note of sadness.

Dael did not answer. His eyes were fixed on an empty corner of the chamber. Something back there was bothering him, and he looked more closely. His vision was blurred and he was a little dizzy. Who was that standing apart in the shadows? Dael stopped listening to the voices around him and intently focused on someone he only gradually recognized—a wrinkled, haggard old woman that nobody else could see. She had glazed eyes, and a spear in her breast. It was Hurnoa, dead and yet alive! Dael regarded nothing but the ghost in the corner, and was about to speak to it, but his throat refused to produce the words. Everybody turned to see what he was looking at. Dael pointed at the emptiness with a terrified expression. Then his eyes rolled upward, showing their whites, his legs gave out from under him, and he crumpled fainting to the ground.

Everybody was astonished, but none more than Shnur, who had cast no spells, and did not even think to claim that he had! Mlaka, alarmed and deeply concerned, raised her heavy body with some difficulty from her stool, and everybody gathered around Dael. Sparrow was frightened almost to death. Dael appeared to have suddenly expired, but in a few minutes he rose with the look of another world on his face, and all present were hushed with awe. Dael, it seemed to them, had come back from the dead. His spirit had left his body and visited the world of other spirits—and now it had returned to tell about it.

If proof were needed that Dael conversed with ghosts, here it was. Shnur fairly screamed that this was definite confirmation of all he had said about Dael, demanding that he be expelled or killed, and shaking his finger more than ever. Mlaka looked quite troubled, but she postponed any decision on the matter, despite her brother's insistence. She stated that she would deliver a judgment the next day, and that was that! The shaman departed muttering, and Dael was led home, his eyes staring straight ahead, as if he were still seeing something other than the sunny light of day.

Dael's harrowing past had burnt his passions dry, and he had since settled into a demeanor outwardly calm and even submissive; but who knew what was happening inside of him, or how fragile was the equilibrium of his soul? When the tamed bird was so wantonly murdered, Dael's surge of anger, always just beneath the surface, was so sudden and extreme that he might have seized the shaman by the neck and choked the life out of him. It was fortunate that his wife and friend were close at hand to restrain him from further harm. Why Hurnoa's ghastly apparition should visit him soon thereafter cannot be explained. Dael's psyche long had been precariously perched as atop a cliff, and the shaman's provocative action had heedlessly dislodged it and sent it hurtling.

While Dael was in his hut, sitting rigidly and staring at the sod wall in front of him, a whisper was circulating throughout the village that he had once again shown his magical powers. Having just physically beaten their shaman without any retaliation except whatever justice Mlaka might dispense, it was noised everywhere that Dael was a more potent magician than Shnur. Of course, Shnur heard the rumor in different forms, and in his heart wondered whether it was true.

The next day, Dael was more like his usual self when the news of Mlaka's decision was brought to him and Sparrow. Koli, who was trying to talk with his unusually quiet friend, was present when the news was delivered peremptorily by one of Mlaka's sons. Dael would have to leave the village.

Sparrow burst into tears. She had been happy among the earth children for the first time in her life. She could speak and have friends now, and she had many of them. Her child had been born here, and had a name that her own parents probably could not even pronounce. Koli, for his part, was shocked and outraged. The incident had been entirely the shaman's fault, and he had gotten no more beating than he deserved! Koli tried to comfort Sparrow, and announced that he would personally visit Mlaka to see if he could change her mind.

The weeping mother held out little hope. Mlaka already knew the facts, the shaman was her own brother, and Dael was, after all, a stranger who had come from far away. As for Dael, he was already beginning to pack his belongings. He was terribly upset, having vowed to himself that he would respect the ways of his adopted people, and control the unruly passions that once had plunged himself and his family into grief. He had lost his self-control, and Hurnoa had come to rebuke him.

▼ ▼ ▼

Koli marched with determined steps to the center of the village where Mlaka lived. The great matron could be seen inside the door, almost prostrate with emotional exhaustion (for she had taken no joy in her decision), being fanned and almost nursed by two of her ladies. Koli was permitted to enter.

Mlaka knew why he had come. She had spent the previous afternoon and evening interviewing friends and witnesses, most of whom told the details of Dael's story in a much more favorable light than Shnur had done. It had been a difficult decision for her to make, because she could see that Shnur had begun the disturbance. She did not much credit the notion that Dael was conversing with evil spirits, but she felt obliged to be loyal to her brother. Mlaka was distinctly angry at Shnur for putting her in such a position, but she finally had decided, with many misgivings, in his favor. Dael would have to depart.

"Come in, Kho-Kholi," she said in her high, singsong voice, sighing heavily and looking to him for the sympathy that her crushing role as dispenser of justice deserved.

Koli bowed courteously. "Dear Mlaka, you must know why I am here—to speak for my friend, the stranger. He is not a stranger any more. He has married Sparrow here, become a father, learned our language, and observed all our laws."

"Until now," Mlaka interrupted. "I cannot allow my own brother to be assaulted, and I can neither pray nor sleep when I must make these painful decisions over troubles that seem to fall from the sky!" She licked the last of the honey off her finger.

"Dael was not entirely to blame, dear lady. You know, he had spent months teaching the crow to eat out of his hand. There was no harm in it. We were all having fun when your respected brother shot the bird with an arrow.

It was so close that he might have hit Dael by mistake! Really, it was a dangerous and wanton thing to do. And what stone would not have been angry at such a time?"

Mlaka was listening and thinking. She knew very well that she would have cause to regret whatever she did. To make a decision was hard enough. Now, to unsay what she had said that very day would be as much as admitting that she had made a mistake. That could undermine her authority, and make her look silly—and all for a stranger. Shnur would be furious, and his eyes would bulge.

But there are two sides to every story, she reflected, and often when the guilty are punished, the innocent suffer along with them. After all, what had Sparrow and the baby done? Yes, she had made a mistake, she admitted to herself, but what could she do now? Mlaka pondered these difficulties for a long moment, and finally said:

"How is your mother, Kho-Kholi?"

"She does well. I thank you for asking," he replied. "She is getting old, but she still has a good appetite, and I always bring her something from the hunt. But as for Dael and poor Sparrow...."

"You are a good boy, Kho-Kholi. You know that I have always adored your mother. I remember when she was born. What a darling child she was, and you look just like her! I remember when you were born too, Kho-Kholi. It was a difficult birth, you naughty fellow, and you have been playing tricks on all of us ever since."

"I will stop playing tricks forever if you will...."

"Kho-Kholi, you know I love you. I know you would not lie to me—not about anything this serious, anyway. And I love your earth-born mother. Yes, she is truly earth-born. Please greet her for me when you see her, and tell her....Oh, tell her...." The words did not come easily. "...that for her sake I will forgive Dael this once. For her sake, do you hear? I happen to know that she likes Sparrow and the baby, so tell her that this change of mind is a present from me to an old friend—though not so old as I am," she sighed with all her heart. "Also, would you bring her this piece of honeycomb? Remember, it is for her, not for you."

Koli said he would, took the gift, bowed most respectfully, and left, quietly rejoicing that he had achieved his aim.

Just as Koli was coming out, Shnur was coming in. Koli moved over to let him pass. They did not greet each other. Once Koli was gone with his honeycomb, Shnur demanded to know what would be done to avenge the insult he had suffered. His abrupt tone was not very polite, and Mlaka suddenly bristled. Everybody treated her with extraordinary courtesy and deference except her younger brother.

"Brother," said she, "my life was simpler before you became a spirit-man. You were always a selfish little boy, yes you were, but since you discovered your gift for magic you have become insufferable. What was the good of killing Dael's crow? It was doing you no harm. Don't answer me with that angry face. I won't put up with it! It is my will that Dael remain with us."

Shnur's mouth dropped with surprise and anger, and his eyes bulged, just as Mlaka knew they would.

"Some say he is a magician too, and his magic may do us more good than yours, for ought I know." Shnur opened his teeth to say something. "Silence!" she said with all the authority of her office. "I try to keep the peace here and you must help me." Then more softly, and with a note of sweetness: "It's all right, little brother Shnurma dear, you are still my favorite. Would you like some honey? I have a chunk of the comb left, and you may have it. There it is. Cut it down and take it with you."

Shnur went out with the sticky gift, frowning darkly and muttering something that was not a prayer.

10 RYDL AND HIS FRIENDS

In the three years since Dael and Sparrow had departed from the Beautiful Country, young Rydl had become the richest man of the Ba-Coro. Certainly, no one had expected him to thrive after suffering a serious wound in battle. A Noi spear had penetrated his thigh just above the knee, and he was lucky to have survived the massive infection that resulted. The injury had left him a cripple, limping deeply and with pain for a long while. The pain had departed except when moist weather brought it out, but the limp remained. Rydl supported himself with a crutch of his own design, and his physical activities were limited. He could fish if he managed to hobble to the lake, but he could not hunt or even gather fruit and seeds, plentiful though they were.

At first he was quite inactive, hoping his painful wound would heal better than it had; but it was not long before he got busy. The first thing he did was fashion a crutch made of two parts and joined with a peg, deftly fitted. The upper piece was carved to fit comfortably under his arm, and was padded with a soft fur to avoid the soreness that a cruder support would quickly cause.

That crutch alone established Rydl's reputation as the cleverest man in the village; but Rydl soon gave many more demonstrations of his ingenuity. He found uses for things others would throw away: discarded bones made needles, and intestines or bladders, unwanted by his fellows, could be dried and used as containers or storage vessels. He developed new techniques for fishing that filled the village with superfluous dried fish, and contrived a half-dozen different animal traps and snares.

Every one of his inventions was a source of wonder to his tribesmen. He was already famous for the trick he once had played on Dael. He had snared Dael by the foot and left him dangling! "Being smart is more important than being strong," Chul would say for perhaps the twentieth time, nodding gravely for emphasis as he spoke. (Chul himself was better known for his strength than his cleverness.) "If Rydl were to have a quarrel with a bear," Chul bawled, "I would feel sorry for the bear!" And he laughed loudly, almost squealed, at his own joke. Chul and Rydl were good friends, although the considerable differences in their personalities caused them to go their separate ways.

Rydl, excluded from many activities because of his disabling wound, had lots of time to do nothing; but he initiated endless projects to occupy himself. Where he most excelled was in the making of blades, an occupation that took patience and lots of time. Knives, axes, and spearheads were laboriously chipped from shards of flint or other stones that lent themselves to shaping, and everybody in the tribe knew how to make them—some better than others. The product of the chipping method would usually be a useful but crude and heavy item.

But Rydl's blades were not crude. They were works of art—slender, light tools or weapons that were chipped in rows so neat and regular that the fracturing was like an elaborate decoration beautiful to see. Or an ax might be made from a smooth, rounded stone, which would be patiently worn by friction into a sharply edged tool. Rydl learned to grind the edges of the thinner blades to an unheard-of keenness; and he astonished everybody when he made and somehow firmly attached a carved bone handle to a delicately fashioned knife. The blade was so slim in places that one could see light pass through the stone.

Everybody wanted one of Rydl's knives or axes, and tribesmen presented by way of trade almost anything of value they had to offer. A hunter would give a stag for such a tool. Rydl was kept busy chipping and grinding day and night, and he accumulated much in food, furs, weapons, and precious items. And it was not long before he had acquired the large house of Morda, who had been slain in the same battle that gave Rydl his own crippling wound. Every hut in the village leaked except this one— after Rydl had it waterproofed with tar.

He furnished his house with a hammock, which he also invented. Being of the wasp people, who had lived in nests suspended in trees, Rydl simply adapted their methods to make a woven bed. He soon gained possession of Morda's enormous mammoth tusks, and kept them on either side of his door, exactly where their original owner had; but now they were held firmly in place by an ingenious device he easily contrived. He was extremely pleased to have acquired Zan-Gah's lion skin, which had become Morda's property before his death. Rydl actually cared surprisingly little about his possessions, and caring a great deal for Zan-Gah, his dearest friend, he made him a present of the magnificent pelt.

By the standards of the time, Rydl had become wealthy. With cleverness and unceasing industry, his large dwelling became a storehouse of valuables—especially furs, including deer, rabbit, raccoon, fox, beaver, and bear; but also a variety of dried meats, fish, roots, and grain; and tools and weapons of every description. He hardly knew what to do with all of it.

That was where Rydl truly showed his genius. He opened a brisk and extensive trade with members of the five clans that comprised the Ba-Coro; and in time, with the help of hired men (paid with pelts and meat), he eventually established exchange with the very people that wounded him so badly, the tribe known as the Noi.

That market was not easily set up. The Noi lived across a barren desert difficult to traverse; but Rydl had learned from Zan-Gah the best and safest way. Zan had nearly died the first time he crossed it, but when he returned with Dael and Lissa-Na, they followed a stream that made the journey fairly easy. That was to become a well-traveled route.

How could the crippled merchant travel the distance required? Rydl had several employees, the most important being the brothers Oin and Orah. Rydl had little reason to like them, but he recognized in his former tormentors (they had once teased him mercilessly) a willingness to obey orders so long as they stood to profit—and profit they did. Within a year of entering Rydl's service, grinding axes or doing chores, they were prospering more than most.

They and some other young men would carry Rydl long distances on a stretcher he had fashioned, and bring items of trade with them. The Noi had many desert dainties to offer, and Rydl could barter dried fish, meat, furs, and tools. Most important, the Noi had salt. For them it was plentiful and low in cost, but Rydl could sell it to the five tribes at a handsome profit. A quantity of salt that had cost him a single pelt might well bring in twenty, so highly prized was this rare substance among the Ba-Coro tribe. Except for Zan, Rydl alone spoke the language of the Noi, and that gave the crippled merchant almost complete control of this lucrative trade, for a time.

Rydl had something else to barter. After several experiments, he had learned to raise grain on the nearby field that had seen so much bloodshed. It was perfect for the project, having evenness, freedom from trees and brush, and sufficient moisture to sustain growth.

The grasses and weeds had to be cleared away and the soil tilled. Rydl didn't have the strength for such labor, so he employed all of his helpers in the spring, and by late summer harvested a valuable crop—again with his hired help. They would beat their grain-bearing grasses on a large, flat rock, and sweep the seeds together. Then seed was separated from straw on windy days by tossing it on a sheet of animal skin, so that the worthless chaff could blow away, leaving only the rich harvest. "If only the same could be done with men!" Rydl mused. At his direction, the purified grain was stored and transported in dried stomachs and intestines.

▼ ▼ ▼

No one knows today what an important human being our Rydl was, not only in his own ancient day, but yet in ours! He took a part of no small importance in the greatest change in the entirety of human history: the beginnings of agriculture—for the time was approaching that people would no longer be dependent on food gathered or hunted, but would learn to raise their own. Who recalls today a single name connected with that immensely significant development? Time and the dust of ages have buried the whole tremendous story. But know, you ungrateful and forgetful species, the debt we owe to Rydl and many others of dim memory. Had they not lived, we might not either have lived to see the sun. Yet, why should we remember them? Who will long remember us?

▼ ▼ ▼

The richer Rydl became, the more friends he made—not because (as is so often the case) people seek the friendship of those they hope to benefit from; but because Rydl was genuinely amiable, generous, and curiously charming. Wealth had not spoiled him. He was kind to women who had lost their husbands through sickness or war, and though he had no woman of his own, a number of those of the tribe had cause to bless him. When one of the widows suddenly died, he adopted her two children, a girl of nine and a boy of seven.

As for his charm, probably ten young women regarded him as a marriage prospect. Had not Sparrow adored him? Everybody was the recipient of, and responded to, his innate graciousness. It was extended to the harshest among them, and even as he was getting the best of a hard bargain, he won over his competitors with his unassuming ways, causing them to feel that if they had not gotten all they wanted, they had not been humiliated either. Rydl was not greedy, and indeed he gave away much of what he had. That too was part of his appeal—not merely that he gave, but that he never allowed himself to become acquisitive or proud. Why are some people charming? It is not a matter of natural beauty, although Rydl had that in abundance too.

Actually, people had reason to hate him were they so inclined. Rydl was the sole survivor of the wasp people, once the bitterest enemies of the Ba-Coro, and he spoke with a definite accent. He had most to fear in the winter. With his soft and luxurious furs, he was always comfortable, but when he was warm and others were cold, some recalled that he was not really one of them.

Luckily, Rydl had many friends, some of whom he had made prosperous. Many could pity the foreigner because he had lost all of his family and friends—enemies though they were to his adopted people. And besides being a cripple, which evoked sympathy, he had been wounded fighting for the Ba-Coro. Anyway, Rydl was so generous with his wealth that everybody forgave him his origins as though they had never been. He was even more popular than Zan-Gah.

Zan had taken his place as an important leader of the Ba-Coro. It was generally understood that his had been the principal voice in favor of moving from the land of dank caves, where they long had lived, to the Beautiful Country. Everybody was prospering, and did not fail to honor Zan-Gah for helping them to a better life. Perhaps the effusion of respect went a little to his head, but his wife Pax helped him to be humble.

She too had prospered. She had given Zan a fine son, and was pregnant again. Their family ate a little less well since Pax had become a mother and was forced to curtail those hunting activities at which she so excelled. Everybody in the tribe was more at ease when Pax stopped hunting and settled down to being a mother. But then, food was so plentiful that her abstention from the hunt presented no problem.

Her son was a delicate boy growing to be a mild, charming lad. In fact, he was more than a little like Rydl. When Rydl visited, always bringing a gift or toy, he was the child's favorite uncle. When giant Uncle Chul came with his booming voice, tossing the child up and down, Chul was his favorite. When both came, Pax had to put him to bed.

The boy's name was Impa.

▼ ▼ ▼

As the trade with the Noi increased, others hoped to profit from it too. Rydl encouraged Zan to join him on a journey, but Zan had painful memories of the Noi. When he had last seen them they were trying to kill him, and he still had dreams about the time he had been captured and tortured. Had not Pax, like a spirit, achieved his release by night, he probably would have died. The Noi knew him as Dael's twin and supernatural double. Surely they would not barter with him.

But Rydl had charmed them too! They had done business with him on numerous occasions, had no fear of a limping man, and welcomed his friends. Their eagerness to acquire valuable pelts and other treasures for handfuls of salt, which was almost as plentiful as sand, enabled the Noi to overlook all of their unhappy experiences with the Ba-Coro—who had beaten them in battle and virtually driven them from the Beautiful Country. All of that was past as they welcomed the trader and his goods. So Zan, reassured by Rydl of his safety, finally decided to make the visit.

Eventually everybody was profiting from this trade; but one who had other reasons for contacting the Noi was Chul's wife, Siraka-Finaka. She was closely observing the new commercial developments, and wondering what use could be made of them. Hers had been almost the only voice for peace in the days when battles were being fought between her people and theirs. It is never easy to cry for peace when all around you are beating the drums of war, but Siraka-Finaka was a strong-minded and independent thinker then—and still was now.

Although Siraka-Finaka was short and very fat, and travel was difficult for her, she started to accompany Rydl and his helpers on their trading expeditions, leaving her husband behind to stay with their children. Chul would not do as a companion, not at all! His giant's bulk was frightening and warlike, and would defeat her purpose before she was able to state it. Rydl didn't want Chul along for similar reasons; his friendly reception depended upon avoiding challenging or aggressive semblance. Rydl was a master of benign appearance, but Chul could never be seen as anything but a threat. Chul couldn't help it. Not only his huge size, but also his almost savage gravel voice was against him. Siraka would arrive with gifts, but without her alarming mate.

While Rydl was attending to his exchanges, Siraka-Finaka was making friends with the Noi women, and soon found herself within the cave of the Na order. The Na were a sequestered society of women whose function, as Lissa-Na's had been, was to attend to births and deaths, and to heal the sick. (They also instructed girls on the duties and mysteries of marriage.) What Siraka proposed was no less than the healing of the breach that had rent apart the two peoples, hers and theirs. Rydl had already begun the process, but Siraka's aim could not be fully accomplished, nor even well communicated, until she persuaded Rydl to translate for her, first to the women of Na, and later to the elders of the Noi people.

Thus, Rydl's trading venture became a pathway to a permanent peace.

11 A BOAR HUNT

Of all the savory dishes the red men loved to eat, they prized most the flesh of the wild pig. It was, however, a dangerous creature to hunt. Both the males and females had dreadful tusks emerging from their lower jaws that could inflict fatal, tearing wounds—for these animals were unusually truculent, aggressive, and swift. Most of the time they were easily alarmed, so the difficulty was to approach them without causing them to run—although hunters sometimes used panic in order to make them run in a chosen direction. But some of these touchy beasts would attack when scared, and they were quite unpredictable about it. A wounded boar was truly a dangerous and treacherous animal.

Dael had never seen one of them, but when there was talk of a boar hunt, he was immediately interested. Koli described the pigs, laying emphasis on the way they tasted when roasted, and smacking his lips. But he also warned Dael of the formidable nature of this particular species—at the same time encouraging him to join in. Dael had already decided that he would when he later was approached by none other than Shnur, who, feigning a desire to put their quarrel behind them, personally invited Dael to come along.

Why he did so is not hard to guess: he hated Dael, and deeply wished that the hunt might be fatal to him. Shnur was in fact watching for a chance to increase Dael's danger. Dael had no reputation as a skillful hunter, was known to be a chance-taker, and had little knowledge of what he was about to do. Perhaps these circumstances would work to the magician's advantage, for he was resolved to have revenge on Dael at the first opportunity.

The pigs like to keep in wooded regions, and there were almost no such lands nearby. However, a day's distance away there was a sickly copse. The trees were clustered around the confluence of their own small red stream with a larger one of a clearer color, into which the smaller bled. This would have been a favorite hunting area if it had been closer. Some boys of the tribe saw the pigs when they ventured in the area with their bows. They knew better than to attack the swine by themselves, but they reported the news to their parents when they returned. There had been an entire herd of them, perhaps twelve or more—whole families with little piglets. Many of the red people would have gone much farther for the taste of a tender baby pig, properly roasted on a spit.

The hunters walked all day to get near the area, and camped for the night, determined to rise at the first light. Three or four women had joined in the group to Dael's dismay. He thought of Pax, Zan's hunter-wife, and winced. Pax had outraged the Ba-Coro by assuming these duties of a man, and Zan had allowed it! Dael quietly asked his friend Koli what women were doing there. Koli whispered that they were the most skillful archers of the group, and that they could hardly do without them.

The next morning, the hunting party rose early, while it was still misty. The rising sun was a red globe, weakened by the fog and tolerable to the eye. Shnur's old limbs were stiffened by a night in the cold, moist air, and he was moving slowly. He wasn't really needed, and several of the group wondered why he had come along. Shnur had not been on a hunting expedition in years. But the hunters were busy, hastening in complete silence to ready themselves and their weapons, and did not care about the shaman's presence. By the time the vapor dispersed, they were already on the march.

The crimson hunters knew the region well. It was a thorny place. Many of the black trees had clusters of fierce-looking thorns growing on their trunks and branches that had to be carefully avoided. The party had only to locate their quarry, which the light-footed females quickly accomplished. Then, hearing their report, the preparations began. Some of the hunters would be waiting near the river, ready to strike if the animals could be forced into the water. Once there, the swine would be slowed down and extremely vulnerable. A large net was to be put up between two trees to screen the pigs from the smaller stream and snare any of them that ran in that direction. On a third side several fires were being built, using some rotten materials that would produce a smelly smoke, but they would not be lit until stealthy hunters had approached their quarry.

The wild pigs seemed peaceable enough before they noticed the hunters. They were noisily grumbling and burrowing for roots with their noses and teeth. The archers struck abruptly, hitting four of the pigs at once. None of the animals fell, however. They ran in every direction, grunting and squealing. Usually, arrows killed by slow hemorrhage, not by sudden shock—unless the heart was directly hit, and that rarely happened. An arrow in the lung would kill, but not right away.

The hunters, including Dael, kept on shooting, driving two of the wounded animals into the net where they became entangled and could be slaughtered. Others were running at high speed in the direction of the thickest brush, with Dael's two wolves snapping at their heels. A trail of blood showed where they had hidden, and the wolves easily followed the scent. The now fallen swine were panting heavily and almost dead, unable to resist the attacks of Dael's eager pets. No further efforts were needed to subdue them, but it was best to keep some distance away, or end any danger with the blow of a club.

Dael shouldered his bow, and approached the net with his spear. The smoke had not served much purpose, but it was blowing in his direction and obscured his vision for a moment. Nearby, through the smoke, he had a glimpse of the spirit-man, who was marking Dael's every move with blazing eyes as if waiting for something. The wind suddenly blew the smoke in another direction, and all at once Dael could see speeding toward him an enormous black boar. It had four arrows in its massive shoulders, which had not succeeded in bringing the beast down, but merely served to infuriate it. Its frightful tusks were ready to tear anything in its path. Everybody, including Shnur, ran for cover, the aging shaman surprising himself by leaping up to the lower branch of a tree (which luckily was not a thorny one). Koli, too, dodged the onslaught of the raving animal, while the wolves, which might have defended Dael, were occupied elsewhere. All eyes were on the man under attack.

Dael and the huge animal had something in common: neither had any concern for his personal danger, but was determined to confront his opponent. In a perilous situation, few men alive had more composure than Dael. He faced the wounded and enraged animal without blinking, merely observing it closely and awaiting its charge. Someone shot a fifth arrow into the boar's bristled hide with no apparent effect. The boar glared at Dael for a moment, pausing to pant, then lunged at him with its massive head lowered.

Dael readied his spear, his lips compressed with resolution and his eyes intently focused on every movement. Had there been three boars, Dael would not have fled. "We don't run from animals, we eat them," he could hear his father say as he thrust his spear into the back of the oncoming monster's neck, bringing it down at last with a squealing groan. Spectators said afterwards that Dael almost smiled as he drove the pointed weapon deep into the animal's body. Everybody was amazed by his steadfast courage.

"Dael-Gah!" the victor thought to himself, remembering his twin brother's name of honor. But Zan-Gah had confronted a lion, Dael reflected. This was only a large pig.

12 THE SHAMAN

One unlucky youth had been hurt in the chase. A wounded boar, seemingly dead, had gashed his leg. It was an easy mistake for anyone to make; the animal had lain absolutely still, and the lad thought it would be safe to approach. But it suddenly got up, furiously slashed at him with a tusk, and ran off to die somewhere in the woods. The injured fellow, whose name was Ta, had to be carried home, along with the four animals they had killed. Ta was in a lot of pain.

When they got back, Dael offered to administer an ointment that Lissa-Na had taught him to prepare. Many, seeing the application, wondered if it would work; only a few had observed its efficacy before. As usual, news of the treatment reached the ears of the envious spirit-man. When young Ta developed a serious infection that was soon accompanied by delirium, his frightened parents decided to request the services of Shnur as well. Perhaps two healers would be better than one. It appeared to them that their son was struggling with an evil spirit or demon of some kind, and the elder shaman was known to have wrestled down similar enemies.

The magician really could heal sick people. He knew how to fall into a trance if he wanted to, and negotiate, threaten, or expel the infecting spirit—so he said. Spirits really did exist, he reminded them, and could do both harm and good. "No one but I can approach them," he almost shouted, thumping his chest. He added that he could counteract the magic of enemies, glancing sharply at certain members of the gathering audience as if they might be those very enemies.

On this occasion, Shnur exacted an unusually large fee for his ministrations—two exceptionally beautiful pelts instead of the usual one. His pride had been piqued by the initial participation of his enemy; and, too, he determined that the larger the cost, the more effective his cure would appear. The price would be talked about, and everyone would believe more than ever in his powers. How else, they would ask, could he command such a fee? The shaman felt threatened by his rival, and considered that he had best put on a show that would demonstrate his power and preeminence.

Shnur gathered all of his dazzling equipment and made a dramatic appearance at the house of the sick boy. He had enlisted his eldest son, Hof, as drummer, and marched to a loud and aggressive beat. He was wearing an animal-head mask with two large horns that made his head seem much too big for his wiry body, and was encumbered with bracelets and necklaces designed to rattle and ring with his every movement. The magician wielded an ornate spear in one hand to intimidate the evil spirit—likewise decorated with rattling items and feathers that dramatized any motion the bearer might make.

In the other hand he held a tall staff, the end of which he had carved into the shape of a knobby devil that looked more than a little like himself. It even had the bulging eyes of his angry moods. He instructed with an authoritative voice that the sick youth be laid spread-eagle on the ground; and with this wand drew a large oval around him in the dust.

Alongside that oval he drew a second in a singular way: Placing the point of his staff on the earth, he marked a dot that, under his hand, grew into a spiral of ever-increasing size, until the figure was as large as the first oval, and similarly shaped. Then, a wonder! The magician drew a turtle's head on one end of the spiral, followed by the addition of four feet and a tail. Everyone gasped as the spiral came to life. He carefully laid two small, shiny objects on the head for eyes—they were Shnur's most treasured possessions, found years earlier in the bed of a creek—and lo! It was a living creature now, brought into being by the spirit-man's magic!

Many understood before the shaman explained. The spiral would bewilder and entrap the offending spirit as soon as it could be driven out of Ta's body, and the turtle, too slow for escape, would be at the magician's mercy.

A third large circle was drawn, with Shnur standing at its center as he drew. It would be a protective wall against the invasion of any other hostile spirits who might attack him or befriend the spirit already lodged in the sick youth. But Shnur stepped out of the circle to prepare a fire. This he did with unusual care, arranging the tinder and a good deal of wood in a magical design, and muttering a secret incantation in his dry, singsong voice. He had a flaming piece of wood ready, and with it lit the tinder, swinging his noisemaking rattles as much as possible.

At this point the magician began to dance to a drumbeat pounded out by his son, during which he frequently brandished his long nails with fingers outspread. They looked like thorns or daggers at his spindly fingers' ends. The boldest spirit might see with what a formidable foe it had to deal! And Shnur's tribesmen would see too.

During his dance, which became more and more wild and abandoned, he occasionally threw special powders in the fire, causing it to flare up and change color—first green, then orange, then blue—so that the spectators again gasped in wonder. As the dance grew increasingly frenzied his eyes rolled, and with the waving of his head he tossed his long gray hair this way and that, leaping over his fire and gesticulating wildly against the invisible demon. He began to howl like an animal or a yelping dog; then suddenly gave a loud scream and fell as if bludgeoned into the circle he had prepared—twisting, writhing, moaning, and foaming at the mouth.

Thus for several frenzied moments Shnur wrestled with the demon, while the wounded youth lay silent. There was something of the performer in the shaman's antics, but it would be hard to tell what was pretended and what was real. He began with show and ended with genuine and deep hysteria. At last the shaman rose, panting and exhausted, his eyes bulging and his face ravaged.

He was about to march away, when something unanticipated and bizarre occurred. As the spirit-man, with some ceremony, removed his mask, two large and noisy crows swooped down on him, croaking and roughly brushing against his face with their wings—and might have pecked at his eyes but that he waved them away with both arms, uttering a frightful imprecation as he did. Then without a single word, he departed, leaving Hof to retrieve his possessions. The spirit-man thought no more of his injured patient—only of his war with the crows, and of Dael, their human master.

The next day the news went out that Ta had come out of his delirium and was advancing toward complete recovery. Not surprisingly, a contention arose as to which shaman had effected the cure.

13 THE THEFT

That Dael was a shaman, capable of curing wounds and contacting the spirit world, was now generally believed, although only whispered at first. Some thought that he was as powerful, or even more powerful than Shnur. People began coming to him with their problems, bringing gifts that they almost forced on him.

In addition, and for an entirely different reason, Dael quite suddenly had become the most popular man in the village. His stalwart bravery in confronting the huge and dangerous boar was known to all, and none who tasted the delicious, gamey flesh of the animal failed to mention Dael's courageous deed. Those who had been present described it in detail, never failing to mention Dael's slight smile. The children greeted him as Boar Slayer, and he was given a necklace on which the frightful tusks hung. Dael was not vainglorious about his triumph, and gave the necklace to Sparrow, who was much more delighted to wear it than he would have been. She put it on Xiti for fun, and it hung to his plump little knees.

Dael's bad dreams continued to afflict him—almost nightly now. The ghastly head of Hurnoa was still there, but now they had a new visitant—the furious, crimson-faced Shnur, with his odd grimace and long, spiky hair. Dael's fainting fits also were becoming more frequent, sometimes occurring in his own house, but just as often striking in public. Whenever the latter happened, curious and awestruck crowds gathered and asked him questions when he recovered about the other world. Dael was as mystified as they were, and tried to articulate the messages of the spirit-land.

Dael discovered that the boar-tusk necklace brought about an inner disturbance that he did not understand. Whenever he wore it he was apt to become dizzy and sometimes began to sweat and tremble. The item had a peculiar power over him, and awakened dreams and fears that Sparrow was not subject to. Still, he had misgivings about letting her wear it any more, and he absolutely refused to let Xiti put it on, even for a moment. And, as if to conquer its perverse effect, Dael wore it more and more himself.

His healing herbs were increasingly in demand, and he had discovered a supply of a speckled mushroom growing in the woodland area where he had killed the boar. These were not often to be found, and he had gathered a quantity of them at the time to dry. His first wife, Lissa-Na, knew of their medicinal value, but Dael only had a vague idea how to use them. He knew that many mushrooms are extremely poisonous, and that he would have to be careful. He wondered whether they might help him sleep more calmly. Lissa had administered doses to her patients for that purpose, he thought, and he decided to try them. He would only use a small amount.

The result was quite different from what Dael had expected. He started to see gleaming auras surrounding people and things, and although he felt happy and calm for a while, this changed suddenly. Without warning or the least reason, Dael experienced an alarm amounting to panic. He lay down shivering, and then in a fitful sleep his voyage began.

It seemed to Dael that he was in a dark tunnel leading to the land of spirits, and that he saw in the distance a circle of brilliant light. He hastened toward it, and within the brightness discovered an impassable river. Everywhere there were bodies of the departed, sleeping or dead—Dael couldn't tell which—and across the river (he didn't recognize her at first) stood his deceased wife, Lissa-Na. Her face was luminous, and her hair was aflame—brighter than he had seen it when she was alive. She was the only erect spirit, although there were many, and she beckoned to him. But the river, pulsating and vibrating like a living thing, and turning rainbow hues, kept him separate from her.

Dael longed with all his heart to talk to her, to embrace her, to take her back with him to the world of the living; but the river was becoming wider, the current fiercer, and lo! It was a river of blood. Dael strongly sensed that to cross the river was to die, and he was seized by fear and a deep sense of isolation. Lissa-Na disappeared, only the fire of her hair remaining, and Dael awoke.

The newly risen dreamer was shaking and gasping for air. He felt physically changed by the vision he had so strongly and palpably experienced. The dream was terribly frightening, but he had seen Lissa-Na and he longed for her. There was nothing his soul desired more, and he was determined to see her again and approach her in spite of twenty rivers!

Dael lost his appetite, and became interested in the effects of rigorous fasting. He discovered that the evaporated visions only seemed to have gone away. They came back unbidden again and yet again. And Dael perceived things differently now; everything in nature made intense sounds and movements. Leaves or grasses vibrated on the calmest day as if storm-tossed, and assumed colors of unnatural brightness. The buzz of insects became as thunder, and he smelled the odors of things that were not there.

The nightly tribal rituals of drums and flutes, playing to the setting sun, became for Dael a battery of sensations too intense to endure. Twice, while the drummers were communicating with the glowing orb—for Dael of a color more brilliant than blood—he fainted away, writhing, groaning, and speaking in a tongue his adopted people did not understand. When Dael rose the first time, circled by a forest of crimson legs, he was in the exalted state of one who had conversed with spirits. None present dared to touch him, and every witness was frightened out of speech. When they finally did speak, it was to hail him as a shaman. Dael walked away with glazed eyes. Only after he was gone did the clamor begin—a clicking mixture of wonder, uncertainty, and fear.

With the repetition of these and similar events— similar yet unpredictable in their details and always unexpected—Dael knew for sure that, like Shnur, he had the power to visit the spirit world. Sometimes these episodes were preceded by a brilliant flash of light that no one else could see. Although his departures were at first involuntary, Dael soon found that he could bring them about of his own volition. Drums and loud percussion could be employed to stimulate them, and various drums and noisemaking rattles became part of his equipment. With trembling hands he used his medicines again several times, with stunning effect. Always, he hoped to see Lissa-Na once more.

Did Dael believe in spirits and the reality of these visits? Yes, he did. He met the departed often enough in his dreams, and was entirely convinced that his extravagant fits brought him closer to their world. And when Dael firmly believed that he could journey to the land of the dead, so did everybody else. He was learning to produce these events at will, and had to figure out how to use them, although they could be very painful and dreadful. Indeed, Dael truly earned his fee, traveling where he might never come back, and experiencing visions that undermined his sense of reality. But more and more, people were coming to him with grievous problems, and he could hardly refuse to help them in their need.

Koli brought to Dael's notice that Shnur was observing his every motion. It became clear to Dael that the magician's overtures of peace were not to be trusted—that he had made a permanent enemy. Dael did not know what to do about it, and for his own sake he didn't much care; but he had Sparrow and Xiti to think of now, and resolved to stay out of the spirit-man's way.

One of Koli's friends approached Dael about his sick wife. All the man could say for sure was that she had been acting strangely since she gave birth to their daughter, and had no desire to take care of the infant, nor did she show any interest in life. Dael said that he would visit with her and attempt to expel the bad spirit so that her own healthy spirit would return to her.

Dael began by giving the lady, whose name was Kreka, some dried berries that Lissa-Na had used for similar problems. Lissa had often treated illnesses that attended childbirth. This time, the berries had no effect at all. Dael returned the next day and her husband, convinced of the new shaman's powers, spoke to her and put her limp hand in Dael's. The mother's woebegone expression came to life when her eyes met Dael's, and he spoke roughly to the alien spirit. "Bad spirit, you will leave us," he said with authority and certainty (although who knew what made him so sure?). "You will leave us! Leave us!" But it was his own spirit that weakened. Dael almost fell on top of the woman, sliding behind her and slipping his arms under hers as he descended. He held her closely, tightly, moaning and struggling as the two intertwined figures rolled on the ground of the hut. Kreka's tongue fell out of her mouth, her eyes rolled, and she let loose an unnatural shriek of fear or pain and passed for moments into the spirit world. Dael extricated himself from her entangled limbs and said: "When she awakens she will be well."

The next day, when Dael stopped by, she was cooking a meal and singing softly to her baby. While he was still there, Shnur came by in full regalia and, to the beat of drums, performed a wild medicine dance around the hut. Shnur had heard about Dael's endeavors, and was as livid as a red man can be; but now he would claim the cure as his own, vowing that it was his medicine that healed the demon-possessed woman. Kreka and her husband knew better, but they were smart enough to hold their peace.

Dael enacted several cures among the red people in a fairly short time. Whether the spirits assisted him or it only seemed so, it would be impossible to say. But it was certain that the sick people were healed in some measure, so that more and more people believed in Dael's powers.

But Shnur performed cures too, often taking time to scoff at Dael's attempts. From a practice of many years, he had gathered a large group of adherents—frightened of the man, no doubt, but firmly believing in his abilities. It happened one day that both healers were performing their rituals at the same time. No one planned it that way, and the houses of the sick were within sight of each other. The general sense was that Shnur's enactments were far more spectacular to view, but that Dael's were more likely to actually cure.

Shnur relied on a large audience—it was an important part of his method—but Dael usually preferred to have only family members present. Nevertheless, the crowd that gathered around Dael was the larger (to Shnur's fury), possibly because Shnur's rituals had often been observed while Dael's were new to almost everybody. Dael could hear his rival's drums, and they, along with his own, undoubtedly acted upon him more than Shnur himself was affected; because their intensity threw him quickly, although briefly, into a trance.

Meanwhile Shnur was engaged in his preparations, drawing the spiral from which, by the addition of head and limbs, the turtle emblem was formed. He took from a small leather sack the two shiny items that were to be its eyes.

These bright articles were extremely rare, and treasured by the aging shaman. They were nuggets of copper or perhaps even gold that Shnur had found in the dry bed of a creek. He discovered one of them by a lucky accident and spent the rest of the day looking for others, finally locating a second by the gleam of the setting sun. He hoped he would find still more, but a week's search did not produce another. Yet Shnur never went anywhere near that riverbed without keeping his eyes open for one more shining stone.

Metal was unknown to Shnur and his people, and reflective substances were valued. Few things in Shnur's dull world shone, and it was easy enough to attribute magical powers to such unusual and remarkable items. The magician produced and displayed the nuggets whenever he could, knowing that the spirit that made them gleam would serve him well. On this occasion they would shine as real eyes do, enlivening the creature he had drawn.

Imagine Shnur's consternation when one of his black-feathered foes, attracted by the glittering objects, flew down unannounced, seized a nugget in its beak, and flew away before the spirit-man could stop the outrage. It would be difficult to say whether it was from a natural attraction to the shiny stones or a fixed antagonism to the magician, but the theft was accomplished in a moment. Too late Shnur saw what was happening, and when he lunged at the bird it simply flew away with the treasure in its mouth. The spirit-man raged, completely forgetting himself and his patient; and the ailing man, getting up without knowing what had happened, groaned, and went into his hut to die.

Meanwhile, Dael had returned home. He was disturbed to see the rivalry that was developing between himself and the older shaman, and moreover deeply distressed at the thought that two factions were forming, his and Shnur's. This was not the first time he had been the focus of division. He and Zan had gathered similar rival followings, and that had led to a great deal of trouble for which he now considered himself to have been responsible. It seemed that factionalism attended Dael's steps despite all attempts to avoid it. Was he really such a troublesome person? For the first time, Dael wished to leave the Children of the Earth and go somewhere—anywhere—else.

Such were his ruminations when, as he was approaching his hut, he observed a strange phenomenon. A large crow flew down from the top of his house and started to bury something. It was scratching a shallow indentation with its talons, placing a shiny object in the hole, and scraping red earth over it. Then, with a single ghastly croak that might really have been the voice of an evil spirit, the ebony bird flew away.

If you want to know why crows steal shiny objects and bury them, you will have to question the offending birds themselves. It is a fact that they sometimes do, as this instance proves. But why that particular crow buried Shnur's talisman within sight of Dael's house, and in his very presence, cannot be easily explained. It must be sufficient to say that Dael noticed the black creature's action and retrieved the gleaming item, realizing as soon as he held it in his hand to whom it belonged. He decided to return it to its owner.

▼ ▼ ▼

It had not been an easy day for Shnur. He was genuinely grieved at the loss of his treasure, and swore he would find a way to avenge himself on the entire black-feathered tribe. In fact he readied his bow and arrows. But now he had another surprise. *His enemy and rival was at his door!* What could he possibly want?

Dael had no reputation as a peacemaker, but he greatly desired to reach an accommodation with the shaman. He considered that he had come to this red land as an alien, and that the magician was a respected elder of the tribe, and moreover the brother of its ruling matron. He decided that the return of the charm, the rarity and value of which he recognized, would be a welcome peace offering that might put the two shamans on a more friendly footing.

How wrong Dael was! Seeing the shiny object in Dael's extended palm, the fierce magician gazed at it and then at Dael with a look of wild surmise! How had he gotten it? Surely this newcomer was a wizard of extraordinary powers, Shnur thought, inciting the crow's theft to demonstrate his mastery over the nefarious creatures. By the object's return, his rival was showing his authority with the black and evil population, and serving a warning to the owner of the bright talisman. It seemed to the spirit-man that Dael was smirking at him too! Without a word of thanks, Shnur snatched the object from his visitor's hand and completely turned his back on him, waiting for him to go.

As Dael quietly departed, a little puzzled, the spirit-man, in an access of bitter rage, came to a fearful decision: the crow-master would have to die.

14 THE TRAP

It sometimes happens that a stranger in a strange land makes strange mistakes. Dael had no idea of setting himself up as a rival to the established man of medicine, and certainly did not wish to fight with the ruling matron's brother. But these things had happened before Dael fully understood the situation. He little thought that feeding a bird could work so corrosively on the shaman's imagination. He now realized that the slaughter of the crow and the fight that followed were but the beginning. He had made an enemy, and it seemed unlikely that peace could be restored. His return of the shaman's shiny charm, intended as a gesture of reconciliation, had only made things worse.

The more Dael thought about it, the more convinced he became that he and his family were in danger. After talking to Koli, Dael was even more troubled. He began to carry a poison-tipped spear for defense, fearing that Shnur or one of his hirelings might make an attempt on his life. Dael had kept a supply of the wasp men's venom, which he knew how to mix. He had told no one about this dangerous substance. Its power was to make even slight wounds very painful and disabling. Dael did not like the poison, associating it with his old enemies who had invented it. It was hazardous to use too; one was as likely to prick oneself with an envenomed weapon as anybody else.

When Dael told the story of the metallic talisman to Koli, his friend was immediately able to explain what Dael could not understand—the hostile reception Shnur had given him when he returned the valuable object.

"He thinks you are in league with the crows," Koli sputtered. "You aren't, are you?" Koli, always inclined to see the funny side of things, laughed out loud when Dael told him how the magician had fairly ripped the object out of his hand and turned his back on him. But Koli grew serious when he reflected on what Mlaka's brother could do to Dael. This would bear watching!

Dael now kept in the company of his wolves wherever he went. Shnur seemed to be afraid of them—although by now they were so tame that they probably could not be counted on for any protection. Shnur didn't know that, however, and assumed (as Dael and Koli guessed) that at a command from the animal-master, the wolves might tear out his throat. Dael, without naming anybody, spread a rumor that it was so.

When another hunt was planned for the woody region where Dael had killed the boar, Dael was fairly sure that Shnur, who did not like to hunt, would come along for his own purposes. He recalled how narrowly the spirit-man had watched him on the earlier occasion, and now realized that Shnur wanted him to be led into danger. The remembrance of the hate-filled shaman peering at him through the smoke with an eager and malign expression returned to him, as in fact it sometimes did in his dreams. If an attempt was to be made on Dael's life, the woodland would be a good place to do it—either when he was alone, or even while he slept.

Dael rarely saw Shnur, but when he did, Shnur's savage looks told his secrets. Dael knew that he must take steps for his own protection. He decided to travel apart from the hunting party, and quietly left a full day before them. He asked Koli to go along with him and to keep their departure a secret. Dael's main purpose was not to hunt, as he explained to his friend. He was awaiting Shnur's attack, if there was to be one. Best to find out what the magician's intentions were while he was ready. If his apprehension of danger was just in his imagination, he wanted to know that too. Dael was not a patient man, and all this was a bother, but he didn't see any way out of the problem, and awaited events.

▼ ▼ ▼

The mighty Shnur, revered and feared by his people, was an unhappy man. Ever since the crow had stolen one of his precious talismans—surely instigated by the stranger magician—things had gone wrong. What made him think that Dael had been involved? Had Shnur not seen the token in his hand? The thought of Dael's smirking as he gave it back to him blackened his days and kept him awake at night. Shnur felt his own robust spirit losing its force. The more he thought about the crows, the more he was weakened and even frightened.

His magic was beginning to fail him. The cure he had been working at the time of the theft had gone badly. The patient, who had a stinking spirit in his wound, had died in great pain for all of Shnur's efforts. More recently, the rituals Shnur performed, although not aimed at such serious problems, were not successful either. The shaman was sure that his unusual and repeated failures were caused by unwholesome spirits, like any grave illness or misfortune. He was convinced that these spirits were controlled by his powerful enemy, Dael, the crow-master.

For the spirit-man there were three worlds: the earth, the sky, and the underworld of spirits. Lately this upstart magician had found Shnur's weakness. Shnur had never considered himself to be absolute master of the sky, and now the birds, its hostile inhabitants, were under the stranger's control. And the crow-master apparently had gained ascendancy in the other two regions as well! What else could explain Shnur's loss of effectiveness in every cure or magic he attempted?

When the spirit-man was alone, he cast spell after spell, hoping he could cause Dael to sicken or have an accident and suddenly die. Squatting in his hut, he drew diagrams and arranged bones, burnt foul-smelling powders, and pointed all of his flint-tipped arrows in the direction of his enemy's house. Those who passed close to Shnur's dwelling could vaguely hear his low-pitched, moaning hymns to the shades, and smell the disgusting vapors. But none of Shnur's efforts had the least effect on Dael, whom his sons reported to be in excellent health and high spirits. The embittered old magician increasingly doubted the potency of his medicine; and could not rid himself of the idea that the shiny charm somehow had been tampered with by his rival.

Shnur decided to talk to his sister once again. Mlaka could still get rid of Dael if she wanted to, but somehow, oddly, perversely, she did not! Maybe Dael's medicine had affected her too, and caused her strong will to succumb. Perhaps another visit would reveal something of that kind. This time Shnur resolved to be polite and even ingratiating in her presence. He would not give the matron any excuse to reject his request.

Mlaka was lying on a bed of rich furs when the spirit-man was announced. No one else in the tribe owned furs of such luxuriance—long-haired, soft, and multicolored. The obese matron did not get up when her brother entered. Shnur bowed humbly and asked his sister whether he could speak to her about the crow-master. With an impatient expression, a heavy sigh, and the shifting of her great weight, Mlaka said that he could.

She propped her head on her hand and got ready to listen, but the subject was a sore point with her. Only with difficulty had she come to a decision concerning Dael. She had reversed that decision on the same day before the entire tribe, and now no doubt Shnur wanted her to unsay in a third decree what she had said in the second. It could not be done, even if she wanted to. And she didn't want to.

"Dear sister," the magician began (and how it irked him to grovel before her), "the new magician is causing trouble with his cures. The spirits that have always been favorable are turning against us...."

Mlaka did not allow her brother to finish. She had heard some good things about Dael's medicine. "It is you who is causing the trouble, Shnurma. If the visitor has made friends with the crows (who have always been our neighbors), it does us no harm, and may do us good one day. When you shot Dael's special crow with an arrow, you made enemies of all their croaking brethren—and why?"

Shnur did not succeed in saying one word in answer to her question, although he had many to offer.

"Because you are afraid Dael might be a better shaman than you! What is wrong with having two shamans instead of only one? Then when you die" (here she whispered and looked around the room), "there will be someone to come after you and help our people."

"Dear sister," Shnur replied, struggling to keep his temper, "I fear that I will be gone sooner than you think! Every day that wicked man casts spells against me, and I feel that I am losing my influence with the lower world even as his increases!"

"Can it be," Mlaka said with a note of genuine puzzlement in her tone, "that the handsome young man has intimidated you? You are the leading male among our people, as you keep telling us. And now you expect me to defend you against the newcomer? You were the offender, not he, when you killed the crow...."

"I don't think the black fiend is dead...."

"...and now I am to come to your rescue? If you can't punish him with your spells (not that he has done anything), why should I? Our rules of hospitality, as ancient as our people, require that we welcome the stranger. Besides," she added in her soprano voice, "I like his wife."

Shnur's bulging eyeballs told Mlaka that she was going too far. She was often at odds with her younger brother, but she really loved him. Indeed, Mlaka was generally known for her loving heart. She softened her speech and said: "Did you enjoy the honey I gave you, Shnurma?"

"Shnurma" did not answer. He turned furiously and left. "She gave me permission to punish him," was his parting and unspoken thought.

▼ ▼ ▼

While Dael and Koli were tramping to the isolated woodland, they had time to exchange thoughts about Shnur, and became more and more convinced that something had to be done. They made plans and discussed their preparations. They already knew the area well and could take into account the lay of the land.

"And now, Koli, I have something to show you, and you can help me, but you must promise not to laugh with that bray of yours and give our strategies away."

It was already getting dark when their work was finished. The two camped some distance from the spot that would be favored by the hunters—whose party would soon be arriving. Dael was glad to have Koli with him. It would be safer to sleep, and the wolves would be tied nearby to discourage assassins and warn against them.

Fortunately, no one disturbed their sleep. The hunters, weary from travel, had pitched camp immediately. The spirit-man and his two sons were with them, tired as everyone else—especially Shnur, who led a life of ease and was unused to long treks. Shnur wondered privately where Dael was, and was quite exasperated by his absence; but Dael and Koli made their appearance early in the morning, acting as if they had gotten lost. Shnur secretly rejoiced that his foe was there to fall into his trap.

The hunt would be for deer or boar. Quiet would be necessary, especially for deer, if the shy animals were not to be driven off. The hunting band was too large to stay together, so smaller groups parted in three different directions. Dael and Koli went toward the sun, and soon split apart from each other in their search. A new, unexpected commotion among the crows, which seemed to have joined the hunters, caused Dael to turn. He grimly observed that Shnur and his sons, Hof and Mun, were quietly trailing him. Dael was grateful to the black birds for their warning. Armed with both bow and spear, Dael pretended not to notice his pursuers. He affected to be thoroughly involved in his search for game, and deliberately led his foes on. The other hunters were well in the distance—as had been planned.

After a time, Dael paused by a thorny black tree. The wolves were sniffing around somewhere in the woods, useless; but the crows were screeching hysterically overhead when Shnur's attack came. With a *woosh* and *thunk*, an arrow embedded itself in the tree and vibrated among the spiky thorns hardly a hand's width from Dael's head. The crows shrieked and croaked their alarm, stirring and beating their dark wings. Dael looked in the direction from which the arrow came and saw the spirit-man reloading his weapon, a cruel and determined look in his eyes. Dael speedily turned around the tree for shelter, and suddenly ran with all his might toward a nearby thicket. Shnur and his sons followed.

Dael had been anticipating an assault, but he was not expecting three attackers. Another arrow whizzed by, terribly close. Dael continued his flight, leaped over a depression in the ground, and hid as best he could. He was being torn by thorns, but so were his assailants. Shnur growled something at Hof and Mun, and they branched off to the left and right, grasping their bows. The furious magician was advancing on the run, another arrow ready. The crow-master would not escape him, he thought, however many of the evil birds he summoned.

In his eagerness to strike his enemy dead, Shnur was possibly a little careless, for suddenly he dropped both bow and arrow, screamed in a high-pitched wail, and found himself hanging by one leg from a young tree that bent under his weight so that his head nearly touched the ground. He was completely helpless, unable to do anything but flail around and angrily call for help.

Dael had foreseen an assassination attempt, and had taken measures in advance. Those measures worked to perfection. The trick was to get the magician to step in the right place. He had led Shnur and his sons where one of them would be sure to trigger the trap. Indeed, three assailants were better than one—since the likelihood was increased that the pre-set device would interrupt their attack.

It was Rydl's snare. Rydl, Dael's former enemy, who mastered the art of making animal traps, had once used the same trick on Dael. Dael had always remembered the humiliating event. On that occasion, he had stepped just where Rydl wanted him to, and hung by his foot in the oversized snare until Oin and Orah finally got him down. For many months Dael, full of resentment, had plotted revenge against Rydl; but he had to admit that Rydl's scheme had succeeded and that he, Dael, had deserved what he got for continually bothering the lad.

Now Dael could use what he had learned. If Rydl had been there at that moment, Dael certainly would have thanked him! The tree had been bent down, with the help of Koli's considerable strength, and a noose (Rydl much later had shown Dael how to tie one) was hidden under leaves and dirt. The moment the precarious release was kicked, the pursuer—Shnur—would be trapped.

So it happened. Shnur was yelling for help at the top of his voice, and his two sons came running. They looked stupidly at their upside-down parent, not knowing what to do, and then looked blankly at each other. Shnur cursed them violently as they began trying to extricate his lassoed foot without dropping their father on his head. They were perplexed, getting in each other's way, and not knowing how best to proceed. They had their bows over their shoulders and were somehow poking each other in their attempts to disengage the snare. Meanwhile, Shnur was roaring ineffectual orders at them.

That was when Dael came out of hiding with his spear in his hand. Its stone point was anointed with the red venom of the wasp men—a virulent and lightning-fast poison. Dael well knew its disabling power. The wasp men, a warlike people, relied on it when they preyed on their neighbors, incapacitating their victims to make slaves of them. Indeed, they were like hornets with terrible stings. Wise in the ways of war, the wasp people were foolish in the things that made for peace and true prosperity. Their own internal dissension, born of arrogance and shortsighted greed, led them to their destruction.

Both Dael and his twin brother, Zan-Gah, had felt the paralyzing pain of this poison. Both had been the prisoners of the wasp men; but it was Zan who discovered, and brought back to the Ba-Coro, the secret of making it. How dispirited, dismayed, the wasp invaders were to find that their opponents in war had uncovered their secret! Later, Dael had learned all about it from his twin.

Dael jabbed the oldest son first, penetrating the skin of his thigh, and then the second. Deep wounds were not needed. Neither knew what had happened; only that each was in excruciating pain and could not move the wounded limb.

Dael could have killed all three of his now helpless assailants, and while Shnur hung upside down before him, Dael had time to debate in his mind whether he should. These men would always be a danger to him, and perhaps it would be best to end their troublesome existence now that he had them in his power.

There was a time when Dael would have done exactly that without compunction; but he had lost his taste for blood. Hurnoa's ghost had taught him the lasting consequences of killing. Perhaps he also reflected that these men were the kinsmen of Mlaka, the beloved matron of the tribe. Their deaths could be justified, since they had sought his, but what would happen to Dael and his family once he had killed them? Would any of them survive the anger of the red people?

"Get up, you fools!" Shnur screamed in fury, "Get up!" But he saw that he was at the mercy of his rival. Dara and Nata, attracted by the noise and full of animal curiosity about the dangling magician, poked and sniffed at him. There was animal fat in Shnur's paint that interested them, and they licked his face. "Get up!" he screamed, terrified. "Get them away from me."

Dael did not hate the spirit-man, and at that moment even felt pity for him. Dael was more than a little puzzled how all the trouble began. But he knew that he had to teach Shnur a lesson, as once he had been taught; so he introduced Shnur to this new "medicine" by jabbing him in the buttocks with his pointy weapon. It was a shallow wound, but it was enough. Shnur would remember forever the potency of Dael's "magic." Dael rejoined the hunting party, leaving his adversaries to recover when they could.

Shnur was unconscious when Koli found the three men. He was able to lift the gaunt spirit-man in his strong arms and release him, leaving him to lie on the ground with his sons. Koli caught up with Dael, and they left as soon as they could gather a few things. After a painful time, Shnur and his sons rejoined the group too, hoping not to have another encounter with their potent enemy.

"His cursed magic is more powerful, far more powerful than mine," Shnur ruefully admitted to himself. As if to confirm the spirit-man's thought, three crows croaked maliciously from nearby trees.

Ignoring his shadowy enemies, Shnur inquired where Kho-Kholi and "the other" had gone. Someone told him that they had left after picking some red, speckled mushrooms. Dael seemed to have some use for them, they said. They recalled that the last time they had entered the region, Dael did the same thing.

The magician, with a savage glint in his eye, gathered a large number of them himself. He did not know what they were, but he intended to find out.

15 A VISITOR

The attempt on Dael's life was not generally known, and Dael asked Koli to keep it so for a while. Perhaps later he would send Koli as an emissary to the spirit-man to negotiate a peace. Dael wanted nothing that Shnur had. Why should the man feel threatened by him?

One morning soon after, there was a great hubbub in the village. A visitor had come with gifts and goods. He was a likable fellow, even if he could not speak the language, and hobbled around supported by a stick. Evidently he was a man of some stature, for he was curiously and yet elegantly dressed, and had been carried on a stretcher by four young men. Although supine when he arrived, he was obviously in command of the party, giving directions and enjoying immediate response to them. The group was encircled by a clicking and laughing crowd, just as Dael and Sparrow had been when they first came to the red country. Two chieftains, sent by Mlaka as soon as she became aware of the arrivals, greeted them with politeness and ceremony. Rydl (for it was he) did not offer the gifts himself, but instructed Oin and Orah to lay them before the chieftains, who seemed delighted with the goods.

When Dael first saw Rydl, he did not recognize him, and certainly Rydl didn't know the crimson personage that once had been his foe. Maybe it was because Dael was standing among a number of red-painted people. But Sparrow knew Rydl at once. She had an impulse to run to him, but she picked up Xiti instead and stood beside her husband. A tumult of emotions stirred inside of her, but only for a moment. She knew now to whom she belonged. Pointing, she whispered something to Dael that amazed him. Dael ran forward and threw himself on Rydl's neck so suddenly that at first Rydl thought he was being attacked by the tall, crimson man—whom he still did not recognize until Dael, embracing him, said something in his own language: "Do you not know me, Rydl?"

Sparrow stood behind Dael, and when her turn came, saluted Rydl on the cheek. "This is our boy, Xiti," she said in the clicking tongue, holding up the small red three-year-old.

How they rejoiced upon seeing each other, forgetting every hate and love of former days! Oin and Orah recognized them at last, and wept to see their one-time leader. Dara and Nata joined them. They seemed to remember Oin and Orah, but the wolves were not much interested. They, too, knew to whom they belonged.

The discovery that Rydl had friends among these curious painted people—friends that could speak both languages—made Rydl's trade activities very much easier than they would otherwise have been. Rydl was invited to stay with Dael and Sparrow, and Oin and Orah became Koli's guests. The others were made welcome too, and provided with lodging.

Rydl's wares were a wonder to the earth-children. Everybody admired the excellent workmanship of his blades. But the simplest of his items was the one most gratefully received and eagerly bartered: salt. In the red region, salt was a rare commodity, but it was valuable for flavoring and preserving meats. Rydl had obtained large amounts of it in his commerce with the Noi at ridiculously low prices—to be bartered now at a profit sufficient to justify the long, hard trip he had made.

Dael was truly surprised to see the kind of man Rydl had become: friendly, energetic, confident, and very successful, giving orders to his servants. He was a little more stout, and had hair on his face—neatly trimmed, unlike anyone in the tribe that Dael remembered. He recalled that Rydl had been injured in battle, and although grieved to see how he limped, had to admire the way he overcame his handicap with ingenuity and inward strength.

Rydl was just as surprised to see the great change in Dael. The ferocious leader of a warlike band—given to violence and even seeking it out—now had become peaceful, even docile, a bright red figure with a bright red wife and son, speaking a clicking language that hardly seemed like a language at all. He thought of Dael in the presence of the volcano, his thundering god of rage, and it seemed to him that Dael had forgotten it entirely, as if he were a completely different person. So much had happened in the four years since they had seen each other!

Sparrow also surprised Rydl. She could now speak the red people's language, which seemed miraculous to him; and he equally wondered at the way her personality had bloomed. That her marriage with Dael was a good one was not the least of his astonishments. Rydl never got tired of playing with Xiti.

Dael eagerly inquired about his twin brother and Pax, Zan's wife. She had been with child when Dael departed. Rydl could report that they were well, and were the parents of two children, first a boy and then a girl. The girl had come only a few months before. Pax didn't hunt any more, but said she would begin again when the new child was weaned. Dael no longer thought it in the least peculiar that Pax should have been a hunter. He recalled all the things he formerly had said against her hunting activities, once thinking it inappropriate for women to engage in "masculine" occupations. He knew he had continually harassed and insulted her over it. "How she must hate me," he thought, but deep down he hoped that she didn't.

Rydl stayed for five days before going home—giving gifts and making trades, but mostly establishing those good relationships that make for easy and successful barter. The crimson people had a good deal to trade. With Mlaka's sanction, honey was exchanged for salt— each substance rare and precious to the opposite party. Far more important were the bows and arrows. These swift and effective weapons were new to the Ba-Coro.

Rydl did not even know what they were until Dael demonstrated their use. Rydl acquired every one he could, and let it be known that he would want more of them upon future visits.

Shnur, still the most prosperous male in his tribe, had stacks of goods to trade, but when he saw that he would have to work with Dael, who was acting as translator, he held back. He finally relented and sent his two sons, who, also afraid of Dael, met privately with Oin and Orah in Koli's hut before they left. Shnur's greedy eyes lit up when he saw what his boys had brought him.

But on the whole, Shnur had never felt so low. He had been thoroughly defeated by the new shaman, and humiliated in front of his sons—who already had shown him little enough respect. The old magician recognized that Dael's abilities were far greater than his. Even worse, Shnur began seriously to doubt his own long-established powers, feeling that somehow they were depleted or diminished. It was the newcomer who could control spirits and make potent medicines, not he!

The demoralized spirit-man continued to cast spells in secret against his potent enemy, but in vain—until he ceased to believe in them himself. He became less and less available for cures and interventions, still pondering deeply how he could recover his powers and his position of supremacy.

Dael had begun to take Shnur's place as shaman of the crimson people. He had succeeded in performing one spectacular cure after another, and everyone was impressed with his abilities—none more than Shnur, who withheld himself from public view almost entirely. One time he actually directed a sick petitioner to Dael, refusing him and even turning his back on him.

That unlikely action occurred when, after the two shamans were one day practicing their art in neighboring homes, Dael's magic succeeded and Shnur's failed miserably. Everybody knew. It was then that Dael became sharply aware that the red people had split into two followings, Shnur's and his own. Dael did not wish to divide the red people as he had split the Ba-Coro; and once again he wished he could leave. And why not? His family in the Beautiful Country would surely welcome his return.

Among Dael's adherents, possibly the one most impressed with his powers was Sparrow. She had seen at close hand his ghost-ridden nights, had observed his trances and his healings—had seen him with her own eyes wrestling invisible spirits and performing wonders. She also saw that he had no desire to enrich himself, and knew that Dael did what he did because he was driven from within. As much as anyone in the village, she believed in her husband and his sway in the world of spirits.

Dael had stopped tasting his mushrooms and roots. Even in tiny quantities, their effects were too violent, and sometimes lasted for days. Even without additional amounts, he had strange, frightening dreams, saw everything in fantastic colors, and heard noises he could not get rid of. He did not need these materials to do his magic or plunge himself into trances. It was not failure to contact the spirit world that worried him; it was that the world of spirits came to him unbidden. The medicines made it worse.

Sparrow was glad that Dael refrained from eating these dangerous substances, and even said so to some of the women who were her friends. Shnur's oldest wife, Esto, a woman who was as fretful and acquisitive as her husband, was among those who heard. She often spied for Shnur, and asked Sparrow more than one question in an innocent, half-indifferent voice. She even affected not to be listening. But that very afternoon, she brought her husband word that Dael was always eating quantities of mushrooms—the very kind that Shnur had gathered! Without doubt, these were the secret of the newcomer's awesome powers.

With that information, Shnur's depressed spirits instantly rose. He sensed that he had discovered something important.

16 IN THE WORLD OF SPIRITS

Rydl was gone, and Sparrow had a good deal to think about. She liked Rydl so very much, and was glad to see that he had prospered despite his injury. But she admitted to herself that she did not love him as before, with a girl's yearning and broken heart. She was a woman and mother now, and could look at Rydl more objectively. Yes, she still liked what she saw; but with a certain regret, she acknowledged that things were...different.

Seeing Rydl had made Dael wish to visit his own country and family. It was his dream. He had never felt entirely at home with the earth-children, and although he had grown accustomed to their ways, and was grateful for their hospitality and friendship, these red people were not really his own. He wanted to see Zan and his parents, to settle with his own clan, and to fight and hate no more.

The conflict with Shnur poisoned his life here. The angry magician had made a clear attempt to murder him, and would very likely try again and again. Dael had no desire to kill his enemy, who could not be openly fought owing to his position in the tribe and kinship with Mlaka.

Violent as Dael could be, it was quite alien to his sense of honor to waylay or assassinate—and these were the only methods by which he could ensure his own safety and that of his family. All he could do was leave, but what would Sparrow say to that?

One peculiar aspect of Dael's relationship with Sparrow was that they never had arguments. Different as they were from each other, there was something in their marriage that was conducive to compromise and accommodation. When he was vexed with her, he withdrew; and when she was angry, she usually gave in. They had never once had a quarrel.

But when Dael announced that they would be going home to the Beautiful Country, Sparrow shivered both with fear and anger. This was not a decision that Dael could make by himself! She didn't want to leave her crimson friends, and she would not! Refusal, coldness, and at last tears told Dael the problem: This was her home. She had many friends, and most important, she could speak here. Among the Ba-Coro she would be a mute log again, isolated, tongue-tied, and ashamed.

Dael refrained from further argument. Instead, he came close, kissed Xiti, who was in Sparrow's arms, and dried her eyes with his fingers. He kissed Sparrow on the forehead and gazed warmly into her unhappy face.

"I have long thought about this, Sparrow," he said in the tongue of the Ba-Coro. "Does it not seem odd to you that you can speak the new language, but not our own old one? You can understand both, but can only speak in one." He paused for a moment, and then continued in the same language: "I have something to ask you, Sparrow."

She had stopped crying and looked at her husband with wondering eyes. "Ask," she said in the clicking language. She seemed to grasp that something life-changing was happening—something that would confirm or destroy what they had together.

Dael's question was a curious one: "Do you believe in me, Sparrow?"

Sparrow told the whole truth when she replied: "I believe in you, Dael, and I love you." This was a confession she never before had made, and she was a little surprised at her own words.

"I love you too, Sparrow, dear bird, but do you believe that I can cure you—that I can drive away the devil that has knotted your tongue?"

Sparrow looked hard at him, as if she never had seen him before and suddenly had found that this stranger was her husband. For a moment she felt amazement and...doubt. But she thought of the many cures she had witnessed, and felt that, yes, Dael did truly have this power. She would give her whole self to him as never before, and he would untie the knot— would expel the demon—and she would speak the language of her own people.

"Dael," she said, and there was now certainty in her voice, "you never fail in your cures. You will not fail with me either."

"Then let us go to sleep, Sparrow. Tomorrow we will fast and maintain complete silence. Then the next morning after, as soon as the sun rises, we will be ready to drive out the demon together."

He very gently urged Sparrow to put Xiti to sleep and to lie down herself. Then he left his wife with her thoughts for a while and sought out some drummers, letting them know that two days hence, as soon as the sun came up, he would perform a great cure, and that they should be ready. He visited Koli too, requesting that he would take charge of his child. When he returned to his house, he put out some items he would use in the ritual. Then he slept too.

That night Dael dreamed of Hurnoa for the last time. He usually had dreams shortly before he performed healing or went into trances. This dream was different. Tossing in his sleep and wet with perspiration, he saw the dripping head of Hurnoa, as he often had; but strangely, mysteriously, her head joined her body, and she was young again. She ceased to be the shriveled hag he had killed, and became the younger woman he first knew—with raven hair, sparkling eyes, full body, and authoritative stature. A new, unwonted luster seemed to shine from her clear and unwrinkled face. She extended a cool hand to his shoulder, and it caused him to shudder, not with fear, but with a kind of joy.

"I have come to say goodbye to you," she said in a voice that sounded curiously like Lissa-Na's. "Enough, foolish boy, I will trouble you no more. I forgive you, and now you must forgive yourself." Dael knew very well what she meant. It was his own conscience that accused him, and she was its avatar. With those words of healing, Hurnoa disappeared from his dreams forever. But Lissa-Na seemed to take her place. She appeared as he had known her in life, with her flaming bright hair and calm, noble bearing, but farther away than Hurnoa had been. Dael was overjoyed to see her, and longed to traverse the distance that separated them.

"I, too, must bid you goodbye, Dael," she said in a voice that moved him to tears. "Don't search for me any more. Love your wife and child."

"But you are my...."

"No, Dael, I am only a spirit. Love Sparrow and Xiti. You belong to them now. Love them for me." And she too disappeared.

The dream of peace was over, and Dael was able to sleep soundly. When he awoke in the morning, he began a day of fasting and silence, elevated in his mind by the vision he had experienced.

▼ ▼ ▼

Word spread throughout the village that Dael was to perform a ritual of healing. When the sun rose, after the day of abstinence, a crowd had gathered outside of their house, ready to be marveled, and indeed already in a state of excitation near to awe. Dael decided that a large audience would add to the drama, which was an essential part of the cure. A circle was cleared, and Dael ordered the drummers to begin playing—first with a single instrument beating a slow and lethargic tempo; and gradually increasing both the number of drums and the speed at which they were played, until ten thunderous and intense rhythms drove away all other thoughts and sensations.

Sparrow came out of their little dwelling looking straight ahead of her and shuddering. She didn't know why she was afraid. Beneath her red paint, she was pale. Perhaps she feared that the ritual would fail, but more likely she dreaded success just as much. During all of her childhood, she had been enclosed within herself like an intricate but inaccessible kernel. Now the shell would be cracked asunder, and who knew what would come out?

Dael faced her without speaking and looked deeply and intensely into her eyes—which were riveted on his for long moments. The drums beat with ever-increasing wildness. Quite unexpectedly, Dael whirled around and seized Sparrow from behind. "The bad spirit will now be expelled!" was the only thing he said as he powerfully grasped her entire body. His grip was firm and completely encompassing, and the two fell to the ground. Sparrow screamed. Dael's muscular arms were under her softer ones in a lock that extended to her wrists and over her breasts. His teeth held her ear, and his legs were wrapped around her in such a way that her entire body was under his control—as if he were a great, constricting snake about to consume her in its overarching jaws. Dael's eyes became glazed, his chattering teeth still holding onto Sparrow's ear. Both were shaking as with an ague. Drums, and rattles too, continued to thunder and grind out their own all-inclusive embrace. Sparrow had lost consciousness, and perhaps Dael had as well, but still he held her tight.

However intense this physical embrace was, the merging of their spirits seemed even more complete. A shaman would have said that Dael's strong essence enfolded her, entered her, and drove out the offending demon, making her spirit sturdy enough to resist it forever. And so, when Sparrow finally was reviving and rising from the ground, freed from Dael's powerful and soul-shaking grip, she knew that she could speak the language of her native people. The evil knot at last had been unloosed in her mind and tongue.

The red audience was inclined to recognize Dael's mystical powers, but these friends did not really understand what had happened. They only heard Sparrow speaking and singing in an unintelligible language, and saw Dael support her as the two reentered their hut. In truth, Shnur was the only one who understood the miracle that, from a distance, he had witnessed.

17 A FINAL FLIGHT

Shnur was not too old to learn when it was in his interest to do so. He had studied Dael's methods of magic, observing him whenever he had the chance. He had sent out spies as well, and eagerly questioned them for the details of whatever they had to tell. Had the spirit-man simply approached Dael and asked him about the things he wanted to know, Dael would not have held anything back. But Shnur, who hated Dael, was convinced that Dael must surely return his animosity, and would offer the older man nothing but scorn. Why, indeed, should Dael share his secrets? Shnur jealously guarded his own.

It was Shnur's older wife (for he kept two) who reported what she had learned of Dael's use of mushrooms. Esto had been married to the shaman for many years, and had shared and enjoyed his material prosperity. His second wife, Peka, she kept firmly in check, almost reducing her to a house servant. Esto told her husband that Dael ate of the mushrooms before going into his trances. The old magician immediately inferred that these red, speckled mushrooms, of which he had recently gathered an ample supply, enabled his young rival to contact spirits as yet unfamiliar to him—including, for all he knew, the crow spirits with whom he, Shnur, had long been embattled.

The disaster occurred on an otherwise happy and pleasant forenoon. Esto, with her gray hair flying, was running this way and that, screaming in alarm and calling everywhere for help. In her panic, she pointed, trembling, to the enormous rock that lay south of the village—one of a number nearby in this land of many red rocks, but this the largest. The huge stone, rising like a tower to the height of a tree, could cast a long shadow over much of the village during the summer months. Like almost everything else in the region, it was reddish in color, although in certain lights it took on an orange-gold glow, particularly at the top, while its shaded body became a ruddy, rich brown. The whole vertical monolith, seen from below, glowed against the cloudless and perfectly blue sky.

A large crowd had gathered a short distance from its foot and was gazing upward, noticing what was taken for a bad omen—a pale half-moon, visible even by daylight, hanging directly above the glowing orange rock. But what immediately attracted their attention, and what Esto was shrieking, was that her husband, Shnur, was on top of that same rock.

How Shnur had scaled the vertical wall of stone was a mystery; but he, in an almost superhuman effort, had achieved the top of it. And having ascended it by whatever miracle, it would take another to get him back down alive. But the spirit-man seemed completely unconcerned with that problem. Rather, he was looking above his head and all around him, screaming out wild pronouncements that no one below could understand. In fact, his frenzied cries were utterly incoherent. Only a few words could even be made out: "demon," "hell-crow," "black witches," and some fearful curses full of fury and grief. He was, moreover, swinging his hands and arms over his head and all about him, as if beating back a drove of invading and attacking birds or demons—although there was nothing to be seen over him but the mysterious, floating fragment of the moon. It was as if he were at war with the blue and empty sky.

This war continued, observed by the entire village, until his shadow and that cast by the great rock had moved beyond the village. The whole time Shnur was striking at the imaginary adversaries, hollering with all his might until, at last, he was too hoarse to do anything but gasp and sob. Afterwards, several neighbors said that they had seen the spirit-man earlier, on the outskirts of the village, talking loudly, cursing, and screaming at someone who was not there.

"Shnur! Shnur!" his terrified wife kept calling to him from below, and suddenly Shnur seemed to come to himself. He stepped toward the smooth and rounded edge of the stone and looked down. Then standing erect and looking skyward, he spread his arms as if they were wings, flapped them several times, whooped one final cry, and flung himself headfirst into the bluish air as if he expected to fly away. Esto's long, shrill scream followed his body as it fell and shattered itself on the sun-baked earth below.

For some reason, no one made a move. There was nothing to be done. Esto alone ran forward wailing, and threw herself on the dead body of her husband. Shnur's broken form was picked up and carried to the front of his house. One of his many pelts was brought forward, and he was laid on top of it, a bloody corpse lying in the sun. Flies started to swarm on the body, and Esto, still wet with tears, brushed them away frantically, swaying and mourning in a singsong voice.

▼ ▼ ▼

At that very time, Dael and Sparrow, unaware of what had occurred and ignoring the commotion, were getting ready to leave the village. Dael assured his wife that they would come back one day, perhaps soon; and she who could now speak the language of the Ba-Coro was not reluctant to visit her family to demonstrate her new ability. They had never seen Xiti, and she wanted to show him off too.

Xiti's parents never got to leave. Three chieftains came to get Dael in order to arraign him before Mlaka's justice—for Dael had been blamed by almost everybody for Shnur's death. Everyone knew that the two shamans were rivals, and now one of them, possessed by maniacal spirits, had fallen or thrown himself to his death. Only one person had the power to enchant Shnur thus, and the eyes of suspicion fell on Dael. He alone had the means, it was said, and the motive to cause it.

The chieftains, nephews of the dead magician, were not gentle with Dael. They seized him and bound his hands behind his back, beating him in order to propel him to the house of the matron. Mlaka was crying when he was brought before her, her face wet, swollen, and twisted with grief. She looked at Dael as one might look at the serpent that had stung her brother's life, and then she began crying again. Alas, the softhearted woman was little equipped to dispense harsh justice, and yet she knew she must do it. She asked Dael to exculpate himself if he possibly could, declaring that there was no other person who could have cast such a spell as her brother obviously had been under.

Dael could only reply with some puzzlement (for he had an imperfect idea of what had taken place) that he had been with his wife in his house, and had nothing to do with the tragedy. Sparrow, who had come along with her baby in her arms, emphatically confirmed Dael's statement. The chieftains, dressed in their red ceremonial robes and looking very impressive, declared that death must be the penalty of death; there was no other way. Mlaka shuddered under the burden of her responsibility. She sat on the carved stool that her deceased brother had made her, and asked if anyone else had anything to say. Koli was about to speak up when another shrill-voiced witness made herself heard.

It was Esto.

"No!" she bawled in a high-pitched, tearful wail, throwing herself down before Mlaka. "Dael did not kill my husband! I and I alone am guilty of his death." She explained as best she could, in words broken by her misery. It was a curious fact that Esto had truly loved her husband. Many had feared Shnur, but no one besides herself and Mlaka, not even his children, had ever felt the least tenderness toward the miserly and ill-natured spirit-man. She had given him six children, three of whom were left. And now Esto of all people in the village had to take responsibility for Shnur's death.

Esto told those present how she had urged her husband to eat the pretty mushrooms, considering that they would advance him in the world of spirits. "I watched him, encouraged him as he ate one after another! Then he started behaving oddly, and seeing things," she sobbed, "things that I couldn't see. He lay down for a while, but he couldn't stop talking—and the next thing I knew, he was missing. When I found him, he was on top of the rock. How could he have gotten there?"

Esto broke down, and Mlaka rose from her stool to embrace the bereaved woman and to share her sorrow. She signaled to the chieftains to release Dael, and dismissed him with a wave of her hand. As the crowd was leaving, she called back Sparrow, however, asking her (or rather commanding her) to stay.

After a moment, Mlaka signaled Sparrow to approach. The matron said that she wanted to speak to her son, Xiti, whose name she knew—for Mlaka knew the name of every child in the village. She also wanted to talk with Sparrow, however, and their visit was an amiable one. It distracted the matron from her grief for a while. Sparrow let it be known that they would be leaving to return to their home in the Beautiful Country—the land from which Rydl, the merchant, had come.

In their conversation, Sparrow told Mlaka how she had been in love with Rydl at one time, and how all that had changed. This was a subject that Mlaka warmed up to. She liked Sparrow (Mlaka liked everybody!), and told Sparrow how sorry she was that she was leaving with her lovely child. Sparrow replied that she had never been happier than living with the Children of the Earth, and expressed gratitude for the hospitality and friendship they had received. The matron kept opening up new topics of conversation, reluctant to let the young mother go. When Sparrow finally took her leave, Mlaka embraced her warmly. Poor Mlaka! Her responsibilities were great, and all she wanted was a friend to talk to.

18 HONORING THE DEAD

Out of respect for Mlaka, Dael and Sparrow stayed for Shnur's funeral. In this land of many rocks, the dead were placed in shallow graves and covered with piles of red stones as grave markers. The broken body of the magician was laid in his scooped-out grave with much ceremony, drums speaking loudly to the red people's gods, particularly to the earth-spirit who was receiving him. A few favorite possessions—among them his bow and arrows and three fine stone blades—were enclosed for use in the life beyond. Shnur's two life-giving metallic tokens were placed over his eyes.

The spirit-man's oldest son, Hof, had a prominent part in his father's funeral. He would soon take Shnur's place as the shaman of the clan. He had not loved his father at all, and would gladly inherit his wealth and position. People saw with little pleasure that the son was exactly like the father. Two people were never more similar, they said. Shnur's family was not at all typical of the generous Children of the Earth, but these were, after all, the matron's relatives, and honored as such. Hof had a pudgy face, a habitual scowl, and a belly that gave evidence of his family's prosperity. While Shnur lived, Hof dared not rebel against his authority, and did whatever he was told. Now he could do as he pleased. For a brief moment, and with some regret, the new shaman looked down at the blades and the precious talismans that were about to be buried with his father. Hof was as acquisitive as Shnur had been, and hated to part with them.

Mlaka was weeping tears of genuine sorrow, and all of the women joined in the general wail. Their companion-grief was not necessarily deeply felt on Shnur's behalf, but there was not one woman of the large tribe that did not feel Mlaka's sorrow as if it were her own. Esto stood apart from the mourners and wept by herself.

After the burial, Sparrow whispered to Mlaka that her family would be leaving the next day. The matron looked through her tears into her friend's face, smiled slightly, and stroked Sparrow's cheek, as well as Xiti's. Mlaka felt a new, sharp loss that she acknowledged to no one.

"You will come back to visit us, won't you?" she sang. "You may stay with me in my own house."

The mere mention of such royal hospitality was a high honor. Sparrow thanked Mlaka and promised that she would come with her boy.

"I will let Rydl bring me," she giggled, and Mlaka laughed too, almost sputtered, in spite of the solemn funeral ceremony that had just taken place.

There was one other person who sorrowed at the thought of their departure. It was Koli. The merry jokester had unaccustomed tears in his eyes as he helped his friends pack their belongings that same day.

It was Sparrow who said, "Koli, why don't you come with us? You can live with our people as we have lived with yours. Besides," she laughed, "we need someone to carry all of these heavy things."

Koli's face brightened, and he was about to reply when Dael said: "Provided you don't play tricks on us the whole way."

"Does that mean that I can't catch you in a snare and leave you hanging by one leg?" Koli and Dael started laughing like little boys, trying to hold it in, but only succeeding in spurting out monkey sounds.

It was settled in moments that Koli would join them in their return. Dael was grateful for his wife's suggestion. He loved Koli, and was sure that wherever Koli went, good spirits would come along. That evening, Sparrow attended the flute and drum ceremonies for a last time, and spent a good deal of time saying goodbye to friends. She was assured by more than one of them that she would be back. A woman always returns to the place where a child was born, they said.

▼ ▼ ▼

Dael, Sparrow, Xiti, and Koli left with the rising of the sun. Dara and Nata followed, loping this way and that, and sniffing as they went. The early parting had been unattended, except by Koli's mother, who had risen early to bid them farewell—but not before having exacted a promise from the travelers that they would come back to visit, and bring Kho-Kholi with them. The parting family had been loved in the village, even the wolves, but especially Sparrow and her Xiti.

With Koli and their pets they were six. They had only walked a little while—the tall red rock from which Shnur had fallen or jumped still visible—when thundering tympani saluted them in the clicking language of which the drums, in capable hands, were capable. These were messages of celebration, friendship, and farewell; and at that moment Dael knew that one day he would indeed return to visit old friends.

▼ ▼ ▼

Sparrow did not at first realize where they were going, but soon recognized that they were heading in exactly the wrong direction.

"Where are we going, Dael?" she asked in the clicking language of the red men.

"Speak your own tongue now, Sparrow," he replied sharply. "It is new to you and you must practice it constantly to make it fully yours."

"But where are we going, Dael?" Koli repeated.

"Koli, maybe you should go back home. We will stop for you in a few days. I only now have seen that I must visit the grave of my wife."

Koli said that he would continue with Dael because he might be needed. Travel was always safer in larger groups. He dropped back a little, however, because of the unfortunate way Dael had expressed himself. He sensed that there might be friction between his friends, and he didn't want to be in the middle of it.

"Dael," Sparrow said gently, "*I* am your wife, not Lissa-Na." There was a slight note of reproof in her voice— enough to show that her feelings were wounded. She was hurt because she knew she could never be for Dael what Lissa-Na had been. Even if she was not ugly, she could never approach Lissa's radiant beauty or her intelligence. But she, Sparrow, was the mother of his child.

"Of course you are my wife, Sparrow," Dael said, realizing that his words were hurtful. "It is just that I need to visit her one last time. I could have left you and Xiti behind for several days, and made the trip by myself, but I wanted you to come along. I won't deny that I loved Lissa-Na, but now you must help me put those feelings and that life away forever. It is something I have to do, and I need you and Xiti to be there with me."

Sparrow, the shy, dumb girl; Sparrow, the chatterbox; Sparrow, the mother of Dael's son, had grown in wisdom and restraint. She had learned to respect the winds when they blew, and yield to the earth when it trembled. Wisdom lies in knowing that one cannot always shape or control events. Sometimes one must simply wait to see what will happen—wait, and watch, and be ready. She had come to love Dael, and in the forefront of that love was her respect for him. Her husband would do what he had to do, and what was right for him, and she would assist him where she could. Lissa-Na was no more, but

Dael's grief still lived, and only time, not she, could soften it.

As they progressed, they saw far off some specks that were barely recognizable as people. There were several of them, evidently heading in the same direction as Dael's group was going, and it was deemed best to delay in order to avoid a confrontation. The band ahead of them was armed—that much was visible—and Koli, prepared to fight if he had to, yet advised his friends to stay back a while. The strangers gave no sign of having seen them.

It was then that Dael noticed something that saddened him, the dead remains of a large black bird with an arrow stuck through its decaying body, lying between two red boulders. The wolves had discovered it. Dael knew instantly that it was Kraw, the crow that had befriended him and that Shnur had shot. It was loathsome to look at now, but Dael managed to bury it in a shallow grave, as Shnur lately had been buried. Dael picked up the shriveled corpse with sticks—for it smelled, and Dael didn't want to touch it—and placed it in the scooped out little grave, covering it neatly with dirt and rocks. When the group looked up from the task, the strangers were out of sight.

The roamers advanced at a slow pace to avoid the band somewhere in front of them. The strangers were not seen again, and after three days they reached the deep chasm that split the land in two. It seemed deeper than ever. Birds made their nests on the plunging walls, and flew in its depths with shrill cries to their families. It took a while to locate the rickety bridge, long since built by the wasp men. Over this crude structure the wasps had passed to attack the tribes of the Ba-Coro, Dael's people. What an unexpected, crushing defeat the invaders had received! Dael had fought in the vanguard of that battle, hoping that someone would kill him; and now the memory returned of those death-wishes which he experienced whenever he crossed the span.

He went first, with Xiti on his back, followed by Sparrow and Koli. The wolves balked and would not go, even though they saw the others walk the narrow passage. Dael was able to coax them over. They were reluctant, but they didn't want to be left behind either. The wolves could not hold onto the rope rail like the others, but they had superior balance and went to their master without difficulty.

As Dael crossed, he gazed once again into the stupefying profundity and remembered how much he once wanted to fling himself to the bottom. He had longed to end his troubles and memories and terrible dreams— to feel no more pain, to no more hate himself. Lissa-Na, perhaps anticipating his thoughts, had extended her loving hand to him, and he had crossed it for her. How much Dael had changed since that day! Now, his darling boy was on his back, with his little arms around his father's neck. Dael clung to his son's legs and thought that nothing was more precious to him, and more worth living for.

Having left their supplies behind, Dael and Koli had to cross again to retrieve them. After that, they rested for a while and then marched on, for they had yet a long way to go.

It rained that night, thoroughly drenching everybody. Their oily red coloring did not wash off, but the earth was no longer red by that time, and their paint made them stand out against the changing landscape. Sparrow and Koli were not yet ready to remove their coloring, so Dael kept his too.

They plodded forward for several days, and at last saw some of the landmarks that were familiar from their childhood. They passed the great rock Gah, from which Zan-Gah had received his name of honor. It seemed smaller than they remembered it. Certainly it was smaller than the rock Shnur scaled, or the other immense monoliths of the red land. Trees that had been small were larger now, and the surroundings seemed rougher from lack of human habitation.

At last Dael saw the spot where Lissa-Na was buried. To his surprise and anger, somebody was kneeling next to it and tearing out the grasses. What could he be doing? Dael left everybody and ran forward to challenge the intruder, who looked up to see Dael's furious crimson face and his crimson arm upraised. Dael had picked up a rock to smite the stranger, and might have done it but that the man was obviously doing a service in clearing the grave of weeds. A small pile of pulled-up grasses stood at the side. And then Dael thought he knew the face before him. He paused with the rock still upraised, and looked again…and it was his twin brother, Zan-Gah.

It took even longer for Zan to recognize Dael—now older, and covered with paint. "Is this my brother?" he said as he rose to take a closer look. "Is this my dear brother, Dael?" He fell on Dael's neck before Dael could even drop the rock, and embraced him with tears in his eyes. Sparrow, Xiti, and Koli came forward. Zan knew the woman, and that she was his brother's wife. Rydl had told him much upon returning from his trading mission, and Zan was aware that they had a son. He also had been advised that his twin was much changed.

"This is my boy," Dael said. Xiti hid behind his mother, wondering at Zan's lack of coloring. The child did not understand the language of the Ba-Coro. "Come, Xiti," Dael clicked. "This is my brother, Zan-Gah. He is my *twin* brother. That means we are exactly the same." Zan did not understand the clicking language. He only caught his name somewhere in the incomprehensible sentence. Sparrow told him what Dael had said, and Zan had a new cause for wonder. When had the mute girl learned to speak?

Koli also was introduced. The two brothers spent a few minutes in silence, cleaning and tending Lissa-Na's grave. Dael was not angry to find Zan there. It no longer troubled him that Zan had once loved Lissa. Why shouldn't he have? Who did not? The twins rose and all walked over the neglected, brush-choked area toward the cave where they had lived as boys. Zan said he had something surprising to show Dael, and allowed Dael to enter the cave first. The brothers had been born in its secret place many winters earlier. The hollow chamber seemed smaller than when Dael had last seen it.

By the dim light Dael made out its familiar irregularities, and then the form of a gigantic man holding a huge club. He was taken aback and instinctively readied his spear before he realized that it was his uncle, Chul. It had been years since he had seen him. Chul's back was turned, and he was stooping to avoid striking his head. Several other familiar people were there too— and indeed it was almost as if Dael's earlier life were passing before his eyes. Rydl was resting, lying on a pelt, his crutch by his side. Zan's wife, Pax, was there, and Oin and Orah too. This was the band they had avoided as they were coming? They might have traveled together if he had known.

All looked up. Oin and Orah were the first to recognize Dael, and cried out in surprise and joy. Rydl also recognized the entire group. Chul had no idea who these red people were; and Pax knew them only after a moment or two.

It had been Pax's idea to visit the grave of Lissa-Na.

19 THE RIVER

When Pax, rummaging through some of her things, had come across the braided lock of Lissa-Na's hair, many memories were awakened. She could not forget that her husband Zan had once loved Dael's wife. Even after Lissa was dead, she and Zan had quarreled over it. Seeing the reddish braid, faded with age, Pax recalled how much she had liked Lissa before she knew of Zan's passion; and decided on reflection that the time had come to make a visit of reconciliation—with Lissa, with Zan, and with herself. Zan was surprised when she proposed the trip. He agreed to go, feeling sad to have so long neglected Lissa's burial place.

The children were left with relatives, and Chul was invited along. Chul declared that he would bring Rydl on his back, but it was arranged that Oin and Orah could carry that burden. As it turned out, Chul was frequently called upon to relieve the carriers, which he did on his strong shoulders. Rydl offered to pay, but Chul laughed at the idea and would hear nothing of it.

Why should Rydl go on such an arduous journey? From his childhood he had been a wanderer. He was only nine when he ran away from home and first met Zan-Gah, whom he loved forever after. Rydl's crippling injury, gotten later in battle, had only increased his urge to roam, and he long had chafed at his handicap. How could he cross the crude bridge over the abyss? His wasp people had been tree-dwellers, and he could cross it hopping on one foot, or even on his hands!

Everybody present in that ancient cavern had much to tell, although Dael and Sparrow had to interpret for them. Rydl was so astonished when he found that Sparrow could speak her own tongue that he was almost overcome. How could she have learned it when all of his former efforts to teach her had failed? He was even more amazed to learn that the tongue-obstructing demon had been driven out in a single day, and that Dael had worked the magic! Zan, as well as Rydl, had fallen in love with Xiti, who did not speak their language. Xiti would have to learn a new speech the hard way; there was no demon to expel.

Some time was spent restoring and honoring the graves of other friends and relatives. Oin and Orah went to work on that of their mother, who had died of starvation when they were children. The Ba-Coro had lived in that harsh region for generations, and there were many graves; most had to remain unattended. The group of friends, Sparrow among them, said ceremonial prayers. Sparrow had never been able to say those prayers before, but she knew the words. In saying them now, she was filled with trembling satisfaction. Her eyes turned toward her husband who had ridded her of the bad spirit. He approached and took her hand. Their eyes met only for a moment, but in that brief time, Sparrow knew with certainty that her life with Dael was just beginning. They prepared to go home, but there was something that Zan wanted to do first. They had not yet visited the river Nobla.

Nobla flowed past the cave, a short distance away. They had not seen it in several years. The twins found the tree on which they had sat as boys, and pointed it out to Sparrow and Xiti. The thick, rough trunk was growing on the bank and slanting toward the river. Zan climbed it as easily as formerly, and when Dael followed, Zan lent a helping hand, just as he had done when they were little children. Then each extended a hand to Xiti and pulled him up between them. Sparrow and Pax remained below. They were talking quietly together in the language they now shared.

The river beneath was shallow enough for them to see the rocky bottom through the clear water. Xiti pointed to a fish or two that stood curiously still against the flow. The viewers never seemed to tire of watching the bubbling current and the sparkling, ever-altering patterns of light. The rush of water over rocks, a few of which jutted above the surface, made a low, gurgling sound that was itself healthy and refreshing. Xiti, Dael, and Zan stared at the water's hypnotic passage for a long time without saying anything. The two fish remained in the same place, unmoved by the current. Dael ended the silence: "I wonder where the river goes," he mused. "It's odd, Zan. I always wanted to know where Nobla comes from, but now I want to know where it goes."

"It would be fun to find out," Zan replied, "but we are no longer free to explore. Maybe your Xiti and my Impa will go down Nobla together one day and tell us the secret. Meanwhile we will have to endure not knowing."

▼ ▼ ▼

The trip home was long and difficult at times, but no more than was expected. On the whole, it was lacking in any memorable incidents except for the time they came upon a bear. They were not far from the Beautiful Country, a region where animals as well as men ate well. It was the largest and perhaps the best fed bear any of them had ever seen, with a great, shaggy coat of dark brown fur.

There was a time when Chul might have met the bear fist first, or smote it with his great club. People change. This time he and the others only watched it from a safe distance as it foraged around for food, sniffing at the newly moistened earth and leaving a trail of its huge footprints. Dael's wolves had to be restrained lest they get their heads crushed in its powerful jaws; but the great animal showed no interest in the band of travelers, and they made a wide skirt around it. Its coat, Rydl suggested, would be a prize, but all of them firing arrows at it would not have brought the bear down, and even the wasp poison might have proved ineffective.

Afterwards everybody agreed that it was a very Chul of bears. Koli, always a lover of jokes, said in the clicking language that Chul was a bear of men, and laughed loudly, but only those who spoke his language knew why. Zan noticed that Dael was laughing too. He also noticed that Dael sounded a lot like Koli, and gathered that this red man had greatly influenced his brother. Zan could hardly remember when Dael last had had a hearty, good-spirited laugh—and he rejoiced inwardly to see his twin's restoration.

20 THE MARRIAGE

With what embraces were the travelers greeted! With what delight, surprise, happiness, love! The father and mother of the twins, Thal and Wumna, Chul's wife, Siraka-Finaka, Sparrow's parents, and many others of the Ba-Coro came when they heard news of their return. Tears and smiles fought with and confused each other, and everyone knew that there would be a wild celebration that night.

Dael and Sparrow had finally succeeded in removing the red earth-paint, but everybody gazed at the still crimson face and figure of Koli as if he might be a devil-spirit of fire and mayhem. But one of Koli's broad smiles was all that was needed to dispel the initial impression. Dael introduced him, and for a long time had to speak for him, but Koli was immediately made welcome.

There were those who feared the return of Dael, whose presence among the Ba-Coro had once been so destructive and divisive; but although many watched for a dangerous eruption on his part, it soon became apparent that this was a new Dael. Rydl, who had visited his family among the red people a season earlier, had informed his kin of the great change that had taken place in both Dael and Sparrow. In one way or another, Rydl said, Sparrow had learned the earth people's language—he knew not how. He also told a good deal about their son, Xiti. As for Dael, Rydl could only say that he was somehow "different."

It need hardly be told how surprised and overjoyed Sparrow's parents were to find that their daughter could speak their own tongue as well. They had already learned with amazement of her skill with the peculiar clicking language, and could hardly believe what they also had been informed—that Sparrow had lost her shyness, and was now as gregarious and sociable as anyone in the tribe. It was a miracle, and a welcome one—as welcome as the grandchild they had never yet seen.

Within a few days of their arrival, the general opinion was that Dael had changed even more than Sparrow, as much as she obviously had altered. No one, not Dael himself, could explain what had caused these changes. They had very slowly developed, but the differences seemed dramatically apparent to his kinsmen, now seeing him for the first time in several years. Living with the painted people had, by degrees, taught Dael a whole new way of living and thinking which was generous and pacific; and the birth of his child had likewise wrought a mysterious change in this once most violent and wrathful warrior. All of this had, as it were, crept stealthily into Dael's mind, and softened his once inflexible, uncompromising heart.

Thal and Wumna, Dael's parents, had a dwelling large enough to put up Dael and his family. Any attempt to sleep late following a long, hard journey was interrupted by Xiti, who had already made friends with Impa and some other Ba-Coro children. Dael and Sparrow were forced to rise, and Dael went to look around the village. Dara and Nata, tame and friendly animals, kept him company. Against a hill nearby, a number of young men were practicing with their bows and arrows. It was a new weapon to them, but they were already good marksmen, having practiced incessantly since Rydl had brought a few back from the crimson country. They had learned to make their own arrows as well as bows, and used them as if they had been in their possession for hundreds of years.

Dael stood admiring their skill for a while, and then chanced to turn around to look at the lake behind him. It was this body of water more than anything that made their land beautiful and prosperous. Dael glanced at the shining cascade on the opposite side and saw a doe—it always had appeared there in the morning—quietly drinking. Dael wondered if it was the same deer as in former days or a different one. The island in the middle of the lake was still thick-implanted with white birch trees, but they were larger and more crowded now, and there were a greater number of dead trees amidst the living ones.

Then Dael thought he saw the smoke of campfires on the north side of the water. Whose were they? He was about to ask his father when he saw Rydl hobbling toward him, supporting himself on his crutch; so he put the question to Rydl: Whose fires were they?

Rydl seemed ready for the question, and his face was not untroubled when he told Dael that the Noi had settled there again. Dael had once led the fight to drive the Noi people away, and Rydl had ample reason to believe that he would not be happy about their return. He watched Dael's expression change as he told him of the restoration of the very enemies who had confined and tortured him when, as a boy, he had fallen into their hands. Placing his palm on Dael's wrist as if to restrain him, Rydl hastened to say: "We are all friends now, Dael."

How could that be?

"It was Siraka-Finaka's doing, Dael," Rydl explained, his earnest eyes meeting those of his onetime enemy. "It was Chul's wife. Once we began bartering with the Noi, they lost their interest in fighting, and so did we. Siraka-Finaka started coming along on the trading expeditions, and got me to translate her conversation with the Na women. You know, Dael, that reconciliation with the Noi had become the main project of Siraka's life. She had loved Lissa-Na and refused to believe that Lissa's people could be that much different from her."

Dael remembered that Zan had once said the same thing, and how angry it had made him. That was when he had struck Zan in the face and promised to kill him. It now seemed to Dael that he had been a madman in those days.

"Siraka even pretended to be sick to gain access to them. The Na is a healing order, to which Lissa-Na belonged, as you know. Once she was safely in their healing cave—I can still remember her exact words—she said: 'I am not really very sick, but our peoples are. It is time that we learned to trust each other and become friends—and so drive out our sickness.'

"Dael, her speech that day was the wisest and most far-reaching that I have ever heard since, as a boy, I came to live with you. At length, having gained the confidence of the women of Na, who were much respected among the Noi, she was able to approach their elders. She repeated the same speech to them: 'No sooner had our two people seen each other than we were shedding each other's blood. There has to be a better way,' she said. 'Let us learn from the crimson people, and trade honey for salt, peace for war.' Dael, even the great Aniah...."

"But what are they doing here?"

"Making peace was a gradual process. Eventually she brought several of our elders to meet theirs. She even brought Chul along. I believe that everyone was terrified of the giant at first, but he and the others brought so many rich gifts that the Noi were soon pacified and willing to talk. Now they like Chul so much that...."

"But what are they doing *here*?" Dael insisted.

"That, too, was the doing of Siraka-Finaka. She and Chul met with the elders and counseled them to invite the Noi to live here again. There was an especially strong argument. You probably don't know of the problems we have been having with the Urga tribes. They have been attacking us, and the Noi too on several occasions. Our alliance greatly strengthens our ability to resist any incursions."

"Do we need our enemies to protect us?" Dael demanded. He hardly knew what to make of the information Rydl had given him; but he began to see the wisdom of the course the Ba-Coro had taken. His initial surge of anger gave way to more sober consideration. Dael had succeeded in putting his explosive hatred behind him, and would offer no resistance to the newly established peace. Doubtless, that reflected the peace he had made with himself.

"They are not our enemies any more, Dael. Our friendship is now an accomplished fact," Rydl asserted with finality. "Our two peoples are married." Rydl was well satisfied with the way Dael had received news of the alliance.

"Married?"

"Yes, Dael, we performed a marriage rite between the two tribes, which binds us together forever. It was like the ceremony a few years ago that bound the five clans that today comprise the Ba-Coro. It was Siraka's great moment, and no one even said anything to her. You would have thought that our elders invented the idea themselves! Both tribes now have sworn to intermarry, and several of our youths have already done so— including two of your former followers. Yes, they took Noi wives, just as you once did."

The conversation was interrupted by the helter-skelter and breathless arrival of Xiti and Impa, two boys who did not even speak the same language, but were already fast friends. "A difference in speech is probably the greatest separation between the Ba-Coro and the Noi, but it need not be insurmountable," Dael thought. "Maybe that is why different peoples are always fighting—and yet how well the children get along!" He wondered whether the painted people might one day join with them too. No, he decided. It could not be. The crimson tribe was too much connected to its own red land by tradition and religion. That was their marriage.

▼ ▼ ▼

That evening, there would be an assembly of the new council of elders combined from both tribes. They and their families, who were visiting together, began by sharing their food. Each participant competed in generosity, for it was considered a point of honor which of them should offer the most to the others. There were contests, races, and games to celebrate the union of the two tribes, joined in by athletes who did not yet speak the same tongue. By the end of their convivial meeting, which lasted well into the night, the council had elected a new elder.

Her name was Siraka-Finaka.

ALLAN RICHARD SHICKMAN is an artist, teacher, author, and historian. He taught the history of art at the University of Northern Iowa for three decades. His awards for the **ZAN-GAH** books include the *Mom's Choice GOLD AWARD for Young Adult Series,* the *Eric Hoffer Notable Book Award,* and the *ForeWord Magazine Book of the Year Finalist Award.*